Wedded Miss

KARLA DOYLE

wedded miss

an age gap, forbidden love, steamy & sweet romance

TROY

A thirty-nine-year-old man has no business getting involved with a twenty-three-year-old woman. Especially if that woman is his daughter's best friend. But that's exactly what I'm doing.

I tell myself I'm marrying Cricket because she needs my help. That I'll keep her at arm's length while she's wearing my ring, then set her free when she doesn't need my last name and health insurance anymore. My intentions are good. My self-control isn't.

I want her from the first kiss. I need her from the first touch. I'm going to love her forever, but that's my problem, because I know I can't keep her. Too bad letting her go is the hardest thing I've ever done.

CRICKET

I fell for Troy Mannington the day I met him. I've done everything within reason to tempt my best friend's dad, but he's never crossed the line. He wants to, though. I see the desire in his eyes—and in his shorts.

When he offers to marry me, I jump at the chance. Because I need his health insurance, yes. But I need him, too.

Every minute we're together, we get closer, until there's no space between us. My five years of fantasies are nothing compared to reality. Our connection is more than physical, it always has been.

Our wedding vows may have been for show, but I meant every word. So did Troy. I just need him to forget about our ages, and focus on our forever.

one

TROY

MOWING the grass in the sweltering July heat was a sweaty job. Had to be done, though. My neighbors are decent enough—until my lawn is too long for their liking. Then the nitpicking starts. Comments about the damaged piece of siding I haven't had time to fix. The faded mulch. And so on.

If it were just me, I wouldn't give a shit. But the neighbors aren't above criticizing my daughter to get to me. The last time I got busy at work and neglected the lawn for a few extra days, I came home to find Gina in tears, vowing never to go in the backyard again, because Mrs. Sanderson stood at the chain-link fence and suggested that a young lady of Gina's proportions ought to choose less-revealing swimwear.

I called in half a dozen favors and dropped a boatload of dough to get a six-foot board fence erected that weekend. I also made sure I got the lawn cut on schedule from then on, even if I had to do it when the moon was out. Or in the blistering fucking heat.

"Gina," I call, closing the kitchen's patio door behind me. "I'm hot as hell from cutting the grass. Going to hit the shower, then we'll go grab dinner, okay?" I don't wait for her to answer before stripping off my sleeveless tee.

Odds are, she's flaked on the couch, on her phone and only half-absorbing what I hollered. Twenty-two years old and still enjoying mindless oblivion when she's at home. The way it should be.

By the time I was twenty-two, I had an ex-wife and full-time custody of a kid in kindergarten. Hard times I wouldn't trade a day of, yet I'm equally glad my daughter will never personally understand what I went through.

My thumbs are hooked under the waistband of my Adidas shorts when I pass the entrance to the living room. One glance is all it takes to understand why Gina didn't answer. My daughter's not there—but her best friend is.

This is where a normal father would apologize for walking around half-dressed, or hustle out of view. But I've never been a typical dad, and Cricket's not just any friend of my daughter.

Hands on my hips, I stand my ground, my dick getting thicker as her gaze runs all over my body. I keep *my* eyes on her face. Not an easy job, because she's stretched out on my couch, wearing the world's smallest pair of denim shorts and a cropped t-shirt that hugs her full, perky tits.

I try not to notice how hot she is, I really do. But it's impossible. I'm a man, for fuck's sake. A healthy, single, thirty-nine-year-old man, and she's a twenty-three-year-old bombshell who spends the majority of her free time in my house, wearing an assortment of extremely tiny clothing. I'd have to be blind not to notice.

"Gina's in her room, on the phone with her boyfriend. Sorry I didn't answer when you called to her about dinner. I didn't know what to say." Cricket's eyes drop to my dick—again. Her lips part slightly, and God fucking help me, the tip of her tongue peeks out.

Now I'm fully hard, and there's no way she doesn't see the hefty bulge through the clingy, light-gray material.

When she meets my gaze again, her big, blue eyes are glassy, her pupils dilated. I'm so close to asking if she likes what she sees, I have to literally bite my tongue. Doesn't matter how hot she is, how hard she makes me. She's my daughter's best friend. I'm a pig for even thinking about her in any way other than that.

"You can come if you want to," I say. It's a dinner invitation on the surface, but a hell of a lot more in my mind.

Pink floods her cheeks as she hugs herself, a motion that squeezes her tits together, thrusting them higher.

There's no way I can look anywhere else. I've always been a boob man, and Cricket's tits are mouthwatering. I'd give up food for a week for a chance to have them in my mouth.

"I'm buying." I force my eyes upward, and my mind back to dinner. "I want you to save your summer-job money for school."

The words are barely out of my mouth before moisture wells in her eyes and she pulls herself into a scrunched-up ball on the end of my couch.

I'm beside her in a blink. Sweaty or not, horny or not, there's no way I'm keeping my distance when she's upset. "What's wrong? Is it school?" I know it's not a matter of grades, she's been an academic achiever since she transferred to Gina's high school in senior year. "If you need money for tuition and stuff, I'll help."

3

Fat tears roll down her cheeks as she shakes her head. "It's not for school. It's for—personal stuff."

If she tells me she's knocked up and the bastard who did it won't man up... I'll hunt the little prick down and crush him. Happily.

"Tell me." I dare touching her to slide my fingers beneath her chin and tip her face up. "I'll never judge you. I'll understand. I'm not some ancient old fart."

A small laugh escapes between gentle, hiccupping sobs. "You're definitely not."

My ego swells, so does my dick. But neither matter right now. "You can tell me anything," I say, stroking her cheek. "Come on, sweetheart."

"I like hearing you call me that." Her voice is as soft as her skin, as she leans into the touch and rests her face against my palm. "Please don't tell Gina."

I nod. I hate keeping things from my daughter, but this moment, whatever it is, can stay between Cricket and me. "Whatever you need, I'll help you." Fuck, I'd give her the goddamn world on a silver platter if she asked me to.

"She has a lump."

At the sound of Gina's voice, Cricket and I separate like a pair of adolescents caught making out. I should turn, face my daughter—and the music—but my focus remains on Cricket. "What kind of lump?"

"In my breast." Her long eyelashes flutter as she pointedly avoids meeting my gaze. If she's embarrassed by a soft term like breast, she'd turn crimson at the words I'd like to say to her.

"What did the doctor say?"

"She hasn't been to the doctor," Gina says when another sob robs Cricket of speech. "Her parents have the crappiest insurance you can get. They told her she'd have to pay the annual deductible if she goes, and it's huge. Even if she did that, their policy has garbage coverage."

"Is there a clinic at the college?" I ask, trying to lock down my rage at her parents.

"Student services are closed until the fall semester, and then there'll be a waiting list." Cricket lifts her head, meeting my eyes. "I know I'm young, and it might be nothing, but my aunt and grandmother both had cancer at an early age. I'm scared."

Angry heat roars in my chest. At her family, for being pieces of shit who don't care enough for their daughter. At the world, for inflicting this pain on someone undeserving of bullshit. Someone I care about.

"Too bad she's too old for you to adopt," Gina says, dropping into an armchair across from us. "Then she could use our insurance."

I clear my throat to mask the choking sensation *that* scenario causes. "Yeah, it would be great if Cricket could use our insurance." My brain's already in gear, composing an email to human resources. If Cricket takes time off school, we can hire her at my company. Then she'd have her own insurance. It wouldn't cover everything, but I'd top it up, on the sly.

My mouth's opening, ready to make my proposal, when Gina jumps up from her chair, snapping her fingers.

"I've got it," she says, clapping, then pointing at me. "You could marry her."

This time, I choke for real. "What?"

"You could marry Cricket." She laughs at my stunned silence. "I know what you're thinking, Dad."

No, she doesn't. And thank fuck for that.

"It's a great idea. You're both single, consenting adults, so that part's ready to go. You've known each other for five years, so nobody could say it's sudden, or out of the blue. Just think about it, okay?"

I grunt, rather than speak. I'm already thinking about it. Cricket would have to move in here to make it seem legit. I'd see her every day. In public, she'd have to behave like my wife, not my daughter's plus-one. At night, she'd be across the hall while I jerk off to thoughts of her misbehaving in all manner of wifely, consenting-adult ways. It's a terrible idea.

"What do you think, Cricket?" Gina asks. "Would you marry my dad if he agrees to it?"

My full attention is on Cricket now, as she blinks those beautiful, expressive eyes at me. And nods. "I would marry you."

Every dirty thing I've thought about doing with her rushes into my head. My dick is crowding the space between my legs—there's no way I'm going to be able to stand up anytime soon. I should laugh this whole insane idea off, then tell them my plan.

"I'll start getting stuff lined up," are the words that exit my mouth instead. "Because I want you to see a doctor as soon as possible."

Cricket's lips part and her eyes are wide as saucers.

In my peripheral vision, Gina jumps up and down, clapping. "Oh, my God, you're going to do it? You're going to marry her?"

"That's up to Cricket," I say, holding her gaze. "Do you want to marry me?"

Her blonde hair shimmers as she nods. "Yes."

"Looks like we're having a July wedding." And a July honeymoon. But that's a hard-on and blue balls for another day.

CRICKET

My phone lights up on the nightstand, breaking the darkness I've been staring into for the last two hours. I reach over and grab my cell, opening the newest text from Gina.

GINA:

OMG! I can't believe you're marrying my dad!

I laugh because it's the same text she's sent me six times since I got home. So, I send back the same reply.

I know! It's so crazy!

She sends a string of laughing face emojis, followed by a new text.

GINA:

I absolutely cannot wait. You're going to be a gorgeous bride, and I'm going to be the sexiest maid of honor ever. I've been looking at dresses online. Soooo pretty. Can I choose my own dress, or are you going to be a bridezilla?

Well, duh. Bridezilla, of course! LOL. Seriously, though. Do you think he'll want an actual wedding?

GINA:

Yep. He said it has to look real.

That he did. After agreeing we'd get married, Troy left to get cleaned up. He reappeared looking handsome and sexy, as always, grabbed the keys to his SUV, and motioned us to get going. All normal enough. Until the three of us got to the driveway, and he insisted I sit up front, instead of Gina.

"We're about to commit insurance fraud," he said. "Nobody can know what we're doing, only the three of us. Everyone else needs to believe the marriage is about love. Starting now, the world needs to see Cricket as my fiancée."

In the restaurant, Troy pulled out my chair. Scooted his seat closer to mine and put his arm across the back, letting his fingertips graze the back of my neck. He held my hand on the tabletop. After paying the check, he guided me out with his hand on the small of my back.

A lot of people stared at us tonight. They weren't the reason for my pounding pulse. Troy caused my heart to race. He always has.

Can you find out what he wants us to do for the actual wedding? I feel weird asking, because he's paying for everything, and I'm mooching all his money.

I send the message and exhale. I'm lucky to have a friend I can be honest with. Well, mostly honest. I haven't told her I'm secretly in love with her dad.

GINA:

Don't worry, he has plenty of money. Unless you're planning on going for the royal wedding package, I'm sure it's all good. But I'll talk to him and get back to you.

You're the bestest bestie! XOXO

GINA:

Bestie? You're almost my sister now!

Sister? Think again. I'm going to be your stepmother. In fact, I should go ahead and ground you now, because I know all the naughty things you've been up to, behind your father's back!

My soon-to-be husband's back. His broad, strong, nicely muscled back. A back I plan to put my hands all over, the first opportunity I get.

GINA:

Whatever, stepmonster dearest. LOL. See you tomorrow.

I smile at the text, tap and send a row of kissy faces, then place the phone back on the nightstand. We're joking about what's going to happen, but it's serious business.

So is the lump I found. I cup my left breast, my fingers finding the marble-sized bump instantly. Now that I know it's there, I can't stop checking it. Hoping that one of these times, it'll simply be gone.

The lump is the single worst thing ever to happen to me, and if I could wake up tomorrow and discover it was part of an elaborate nightmare, I would drop to my knees and thank God. But the lump is reality, and now, it's making an otherwise impossible dream come true.

I'm marrying Troy Mannington.

Yes, it's because I need good medical insurance, and he's the kindest, most generous man I've ever known. That doesn't mean I'm not going to enjoy every fake minute of it. Or that I'm not going to try making it real.

There's something between us, and it's not father-daughterly. Troy has made me tingle since the first day I met him. He might never admit it, but he feels the same. There's raw desire in his eyes when he looks at me, which he does a lot. His eyes aren't the only telltale sign. I've watched his nostrils flare when I get really close to him. I've heard him growl when I mention boys while talking to Gina.

That's all they are, those names I drop. Boys. They could never measure up to the man Troy is. I can say that quite literally after seeing Troy in his gray shorts today. Well-formed muscles glistening from exertion, he'd stood there and let me look my fill, as his sweat-dampened shorts showed off every ridge of his long, hard cock.

He wouldn't have had a hard-on if he wasn't attracted to me. He wouldn't rush to my side, stroke my face, and call me *sweetheart* if he didn't care about me.

I know he won't act on his feelings right now. But once we're married, I'm going to make it impossible for him to do anything else.

two

TROY

THE CEREMONY WAS SUPPOSED to start nearly ten minutes ago. The officiant hasn't said anything yet, but we both know he's watching the clock. City hall ceremonies are efficient. Get in, get hitched, get out. I snagged the only available slot this week, so I know another couple is waiting in the wings. No room to overflow once the minute hand hits the six. If my bride-to-be doesn't arrive in the next few minutes, we'll be out of luck.

Unless she's not running late. Maybe she changed her mind.

"Fuck," I mutter, after turning my back on the handful of people waiting to witness our big day.

The officiant shoots me a sympathetic look. He's probably seen it all. Enough to know better than to offer false hope.

I shove my hands into my pockets. "How often do you see the groom get stood up?"

"We average a fifteen percent last-minute cancellation

rate. Bearing in mind, it's not always a runaway bride situation."

I grunt. "Doesn't help me much, but thanks."

"I don't think you have anything to worry about," the man says, nodding toward the entrance.

I turn—and lose the ability to breathe. Cricket stands in the doorway, looking like the perfect combination of a fairytale princess and my filthiest fantasy. My soon-to-be wife. In name only, but I'm still the luckiest bastard on Earth. I'm going to enjoy every minute I get to play the role of happy husband.

Cricket reaches me in the time it takes to resume breathing. She told me she didn't care if we had a city-hall ceremony or a church wedding. I opted for city hall because it was easier and faster. I should've waited. She deserves a church. One with an aisle long enough to do her beauty justice.

"You're absolutely fucking stunning," I say, taking her hand, once she passes her bouquet to Gina.

"Thank you." Somehow, she manages to glow even brighter. As if my opinion means something. She has no idea how much I'd love to worship at her altar. Her lips are painted bubble-gum-pink, and her cheeks take on the same tint as she says, "You look pretty fucking hot."

My laugh is too loud for the hushed space. Too rough for the moment. It's who I am. You can put a monkey in a monkey suit, but underneath, he's still an animal.

The clerk clears his throat, dragging our attention in his direction. "Are we ready to get started?"

"Definitely," she says, smiling at me.

The rest of the ceremony breezes by. The standard vows are exchanged, then it's time for the kiss. The clerk says the magic words, cuing the moment I've been waiting for since

Cricket walked into my house for the first time. We discussed the obligatory kiss during our prep and planning. I promised her it'd be the only time she had to do it, but it needs to look legit. She gave permission for the real deal.

That's exactly what she's going to get.

"Mrs. Mannington," I say, cupping her delicate face in my hands. My dick went to half-mast as soon as she walked in, showing off her hourglass curves and luscious tits in that white, strapless dress. As I dip down and seal my lips over hers, I'm pretty sure I couldn't get any harder.

Until her hands find my waist and she tugs me closer. Then opens for me, teasing her tongue into my mouth.

Jesus fuck. I slide one hand to her nape, the other to the small of her back, and pull her tight against me while I plunder her pretty mouth. I don't care who's watching, who's judging. Right now, she's my wife. My beautiful, sexy wife.

TROY

Gina rode with us in the limo I hired, robbing me of an opportunity to talk to Cricket about the kiss. Our stop at a park for photos was too public. Dinner at the steakhouse wasn't the place for that conversation, either, despite being in a private room. Too quiet a setting, since our only "guests" were Gina and her boyfriend, and my business partner and his wife.

Cricket's parents didn't show for the ceremony or the

dinner. Not surprising, they've always been useless pieces of shit. She said it didn't bother her, but it had to have hurt.

She fell asleep as soon as we headed for the airport. She's under a lot of stress, she needed the rest more than a conversation about our kiss. Then came the bustling airport, more sleep during our overnight flight to Jamaica, and a crowded shuttle-bus ride to the resort.

But we're finally here. Together. Alone.

"Fuck," I say, opening our suite door. "I specifically asked for a room with two beds."

"You did?"

My eyes meet Cricket's. "Of course. We're married so you can see a doctor and get whatever care you need. I know it's not more than that."

There's so much unvoiced emotion in her expression, in her eyes, it takes everything in me to stand there and silently wait for the answer that never materializes.

I jerk my head in the direction we came from. "Let's head back to the lobby so they can fix their mistake."

"This room is fine."

I glance inside and grunt. "Says the woman who'll be sleeping like a queen, sprawled in the king-sized bed. I'd rather not spend the next five days camped out on that loveseat."

"You won't have to." Her face turns the prettiest pink. "We can share the bed, it's really big."

"If I share the bed with you, it won't be the only thing that's really big." The words are out of my mouth before my big brain kicks in. Since I can't take them back, I own them with a grin and gruff laugh. "Don't want to traumatize you when you come into contact with my morning wood."

"That's a real thing?"

"Hell, yeah." So is afternoon, evening, and all-night-long wood, when I'm around her. "You've never spent the night with a guy, and woken up to a hard dick pressed against your ass?" *My* dick grows fully hard as my adorable bride shakes her head furiously. I set our suitcases on the tile floor and lean closer to her, with one arm braced on the doorframe. I shouldn't be talking to her this way. Definitely shouldn't be this close to her. "Does that mean you've never spent the night with a guy, or that he wasn't man enough to wake you up the way a woman deserves?"

"The second one," she says softly. "I'm not a virgin, Troy."

Fuck, I shouldn't have pushed her into sharing that information. Knowing she's not saving her V-card for some decent, appropriately aged guy down the road isn't going to help my control this week.

I push off the wall and grab the suitcases. Gotta keep my hands occupied before I do something stupid. "And I'm not a saint. Sharing a bed is a bad idea." I tick my head toward the front of the resort again. "Let's go get a different room."

three

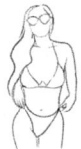

CRICKET

A COUPLE YEARS AGO, I saw Troy slice his finger open while sharpening lawn mower blades. Earlier this summer, I watched him scrape the crap out of his forearm and shin when Gina's kitten darted out the door, and he full-on nosedived to the concrete to catch it before it reached the road. So, I know what pain looks like on his handsome face.

He made a similar expression the moment the resort's concierge informed us they have no available rooms for us to swap. I've never been so happy to see Troy in discomfort.

I got super lucky. I should've taken the opportunity to tell him what I wanted when he opened our suite door the first time. I chickened out. That won't happen a second time.

He's waiting for me on the opposite side of the bathroom door, I can hear him out there. He hasn't knocked, hasn't asked me what's taking so long, but I'm sure both things have crossed his mind. He's not a do-nothing kind of guy. He's always got something going on, whether it's his business, stuff around the house, or working out.

Oh, the working out. Troy has a home gym, and boy, he knows how to use it. I never understood the hype when my fellow cheerleaders would giggle and swoon over the guys in the high school fitness room. Not that they weren't built. Most were. They just didn't do it for me.

Nobody did. Not the athletic guys on the football team. Not the preppy guys captaining all the intellectual clubs. Not the tough guys getting into fights and smoking on school property. Not the girls, either. I was honestly starting to wonder if I even *had* a sex drive...until I met Troy Mannington.

My flaky parents moved us around a lot, as they flip-flopped between jobs, or simply ran out of money for rent. Central Collegiate was my third high school. I met Gina my first day there, in biology, which I only took because mid-semester enrollment meant my options were limited. It was the best class I've ever hated because Gina became my best friend. Then, by default, her dad became the only man I've ever loved.

Yes, love. A crush would have fizzled over the past five years. My feelings for Troy have grown. Grown so big, I've barely contained them. Especially the night of my twenty-first birthday, when Gina and Troy threw me a surprise party.

Troy tended bar for us that night. He stood behind the pool-house bar, serving free drinks to a patio full of twenty-somethings, his watchful gaze never straying too far from Gina, or from me.

"Better slow down with this one." His fingers had lingered on the third cocktail he passed across the bar.

"Don't want you getting too wobbly, and falling into the pool in your pretty dress."

In hindsight, I know he was complimenting how I looked in the soft-pink, body-hugging tank dress I'd bought. At the time, I took it as a hint to get more of his attention. A lot more.

I drank the entire rum and cola right there, in front of his twinkling eyes. Then I fake-wobbled to the pool and "fell in."

The splash drew every reaction imaginable—shrieks, gasps, hoots, and laughter. Troy did rush to my rescue, as expected. Unfortunately, he wasn't the first person to do so, or the closest. He had to come out from behind the bar, then weave through the partygoers and patio furniture, before reaching the pool. Gina's boyfriend happened to be poolside and dove in immediately. Not at all the scenario I'd concocted in my lovesick mind.

I spent the rest of that evening nursing a cup of coffee and a lot of soggy disappointment. Throughout the party, Troy's attention had lingered on my corner of the patio. Because he cared about me, obviously. He always has. As the party wound down, he left his post to join me. I'll never forget the intensity in his gaze, or the sensation of his warm, strong palms splayed just above my knees, as he crouched before me.

"I know what you did, what you wanted," he'd said, his thumbs making sweeping passes over my skin.

"And?" Between embarrassment and excitement, it was all I was able to say.

"And, I see you, sweetheart." It was the closest thing to an acknowledgment of our connection, to his attraction, and the first time he ever called me that. The only time, until the night on his couch.

I'm going to make him say it again. I want him too much to settle for less than everything. He wants me, too. His kiss at our wedding was more than for show. A lot more.

Troy may be determined to keep this trip platonic, but I'm determined, too. We're sharing that king-sized bed in the other room. Our marriage is moving from a sheet of paper, to between the sheets. Tonight.

I issue a confident nod at my reflection, then open the bathroom door. He's not waiting on the other side anymore. He's on the balcony, arms spread and braced on the railing, his heather-gray t-shirt pulled taut across his broad back and shoulders.

At the sound of my sandals clicking on the tile floor, he turns. His gaze travels over every inch of me as he enters our suite and closes the slider behind him. "New bathing suit?"

My pulse races as I nod, and do a slow turn so he can see the whole thing—not that there's much of it. "I bought it for this trip."

His Adam's apple slides up and down, then he clears his throat and grabs two towels from a chair. "Ready to go?"

"You're not going to tell me I can't wear this in public?" I ask, doing another half turn, just in case he missed the fact that my entire ass is on display in the thong bottom of the world's tiniest string bikini.

"You're a grown woman, you can wear whatever you want."

"And you won't mind if some men check me out?"

"There's no *if* about it. No *some*, either. Every man out there will be tongue-on-the-ground staring at you. There'll be enough male drool on the concrete to make the pool seem like a desert. But you know that, and it's obviously what you want since you bought that bikini."

Is he that oblivious? Maybe he truly isn't interested in taking our relationship further, and wishful thinking has allowed me to read too much into things, even the world's hottest kiss. "Never mind. I'll change." I stomp to the bed like a sulky child—exactly how I *don't* want him to see me. Not a great way to start our trip.

"Hey." He crowds my personal space as I straighten, another swimsuit wadded in my fist. "Don't change because of me. You look gorgeous in this bikini. You're a fucking wet-dream goddess."

"So, you like it?" I ask, turning to meet his eyes.

A gruff, grunted laugh tickles my cheek because we're that close. "Yeah, I like it." His gaze drops to my breasts, and his nostrils flare. "Too much, but that's my problem, not yours."

"I don't think it's a problem. I like looking at your body, too. I don't get to ogle you the way I want when Gina's around, so I plan to take full advantage of this time alone with you. I think you should do the same," I say, tapping the center of his chest.

In a snap, his hand flattens mine on his chest. He holds my gaze while sliding my palm downward, all the way to the front of his swim trunks—and his thoroughly hard cock beneath. He raises an eyebrow at my gasp. "Our ideas of 'taking full advantage' are very different."

"I don't think so."

He groans when I squeeze his thick shaft, then plucks my hand from his body, and steps away to pick up the towels he abandoned. "I know so." He nods toward the door. "Come on, let's go make you the highlight of every man's day."

TROY

The wet-dream comment was bad enough. Putting her hand on my dick... What the fuck was I thinking? I wasn't. Couldn't. My brain was scrambled the moment she appeared in those scraps of fabric she calls a bathing suit.

Will I mind if other men check her out? *Will I fucking mind?* Guess I've done a decent job of hiding my true feelings for her, because not only will I mind, I'm going to lose my fucking mind. Maybe it'll rain. Then I won't have to sit at that pool and silently play it cool while every asshole in the place gawks at Cricket's sinfully hot body.

Even now, as we walk through the resort, it takes every ounce of my willpower to leave a buffer between us. She has no idea how much I'd like to "take advantage" of this time with her.

"Full sun, or shade?" she asks when we reach the pool.

"Shade." My gaze drops to her ass. "Don't want you getting a sunburn on skin that's not used to being exposed."

She's clearly in the mood to push my buttons, because she turns that perfect peach toward me and arches her back. "You could rub sunscreen all over it, make sure every inch is thoroughly taken care of."

I grunt while dragging a pair of lounge chairs to a location that will limit everyone else's view of my hot, young bride. "Keep it up and you'll learn there are other ways to get a red ass. You're not too old for a spanking, you know."

Her full lips part, but there's no shock or disgust in her

expression. I focus on spreading out towels, but she's in my peripheral, staring as I peel off my t-shirt. The intensity of her attention sends more blood to my already fat dick. And when she stretches out, stomach down, on one of the loungers, I know I'm royally fucked.

"Troy."

"Yeah?" I have no choice but to look at her directly when she says my name.

"Spank it or lotion it." The sassy little brat wiggles until *it* jiggles, smiling at me over her shoulder. "I'll enjoy whichever you choose."

"Then, you're out of luck, because I'm not doing either." I park myself on the chair beside her, cross my arms behind my head, and close my eyes. Self-preservation. I need some.

She huffs, and I can't help laughing. Also, letting a victory smile take its rightful place on my face, at the sound of the sunscreen bottle lip snapping open beside me.

"Troy."

"Cricket." My eyes stay closed. Fool me once.

Another adorable huff comes from her direction. "I'll give you another choice. You can rub lotion on my body, or I can get another guy to do it."

Now, I have to look. I crack one eye open and find her waving the bottle at me. This is the perfect opportunity to set her free. Encourage her to enjoy this trip to its fullest by choosing an age-appropriate guy to make memories with. Even if I do that by calling her bluff, it'd be the right thing.

"Give it to me." I'll do the right thing later. Right now, it's self-induced torture time.

"I didn't think you'd really do it," she says, passing me the sunscreen.

"There's still time to withdraw your ultimatum." I shift to the edge of her chair, shake a generous glob of sunscreen into my palm, then give her one more chance. "Last call for takebacks."

She shakes her head. "I want you to do it."

"Move your hair to the side." There's no mistaking the huskiness in my voice. Good thing I'm sitting, or there'd be no mistaking the huge bulge I'm sporting.

"It's cold," she says when I flatten my palms on her shoulder blades. "But your hands feel good. I've always liked your hands."

Answering is a mistake. Like every other one, I go ahead and make it anyway. "My hands, huh?" I ask, sliding mine downward, spreading the lotion over every inch of her nearly bare back. *Bare back*. Not a good word combo to think of while I'm touching her. Now all I can think of is bareback, and how it'd feel to sink inside her pussy with nothing between us.

"Among other things."

Not taking that invitation. I keep my mouth shut, focus on her gorgeous body that I'm touching this one time only. I skate my hands over the dip of her lower back, right above the edge of her thong bikini bottom. I add more lotion to my hands, rub them together to warm it up better this time, then make the move that might actually kill me.

Thank fuck her eyes are closed when I set my palms on her sweet, round, sexy ass. She can't see how much I'm enjoying this. How much I want her.

Cover her soft skin with lotion, then get the hell away from her—that's what I should do. But when she parts her thighs beneath my touch, I'm not going anywhere.

I knead her firm, full cheeks. This isn't sunscreen application, it's a massage. One I don't stop. I slide my hands lower, sweep my thumbs along the smiley curves where her ass meets her legs, all the way to the fabric covering her pussy.

"I shouldn't be touching you." I press the pad of my thumb against her entrance, groaning when the tiny strip of material dips inside, revealing a hint of her soft, pink pussy lips. "Yell at me. Hit me. Tell me to get my filthy fucking hands off you."

"Never," she whispers, opening her legs wider. "I've been thinking about this since forever. I still do, every day."

I plant one arm on the other side of the lounge chair, caging her in place and sheltering her upper body from view. "Every day?"

She pulls her bottom lip between her teeth. "Constantly."

Fuck. *Fuck.* I'm in so much trouble. "Do you touch yourself when you think of me?" I ask, stroking her through the fabric.

"Yes."

"Do you make yourself come?"

Her eyelids flutter when I roll firm circles over her clit. "Always."

"Tell me how you do it." I'm a glutton for punishment, making this demand.

"Mostly like this, on my stomach."

Fuck, I can picture it. Vividly, as if she's doing it right now. Something else for me to think about when I'm jerking off, grunting her name as I blow yet another Cricket-inspired load.

"It's my turn now," I say, slipping my fingers beneath the fabric. I slide them up and down through her slick, soft heat. Teasing. Rolling. Pressing. "You want me to make you come, sweetheart?"

"Yes." Her breath catches, coming in soft, panted gasps as she matches my rhythm. "God, so much."

"Fuck, you're beautiful." My dick is so hard, it's aching. I'd do just about anything to be buried inside her. I flex my fingers, giving her more pressure. "So fucking sexy."

She doesn't speak. Just rides my hand. Her lips are parted, her eyes pinched closed, her ass rising and tightening as she grinds against my fingers. Fucking perfection.

"That's right. Rub that hot little pussy all over my fingers. Show me how pretty you look when you come."

"I don't want anyone to see."

"Just me, I'm the only one who gets to see you." I lean over her back, groaning at the pressure it puts on my throbbing dick. "I'm so fucking hard for you. Always so hard for you. I need to feel you come."

The softest, sexiest moan leaves her mouth as she tips over, rhythm dissolving into frantic jerking against my hand. *Troy...God, Troy...*

Thank fuck we're in public, because there's no way I'd keep my dick out of her if we weren't. I hold myself in place after she goes limp beneath me, kissing her back while she catches her breath.

"Tickle?" I ask when a shiver ripples through her.

"No, I'm just..." Her blonde hair moves like lapping waves when she shakes her head against the lounge chair. "Embarrassed."

"Nobody saw."

"You did," she whispers, pinching her eyes tighter. "I can't believe I did that."

Is that regret? Probably. *Fuck.* I should've known better. I did know better. But I went ahead and took what I wanted anyway.

"You don't need to be embarrassed around me." I withdraw my hand from the heaven I'll never touch again and straighten her skimpy bikini bottoms. "We'll act like it never happened," I say, rising to a stand. "Going to have a swim. See you in a bit."

My focus is on the pool as I walk away. I doubt she looks at me, but I'll never know. I already feel like a douchebag, I don't need to see it written all over Cricket's face.

It's still relatively early since we grabbed an overnight flight. The poolside area isn't busy, and I honestly don't give half a fuck if anybody notices the tentpole at the front of my trunks. I deserve any ridicule that comes my way.

My body slices the water when I dive into the deep end. I've got the pool to myself and I carve it up, doing three quick lengths. I make the turn for the fourth lap, and spot Cricket bobbing in the pool, directly ahead. Fuck. I power out the rest of the lap, stopping at the wall where she's obviously waiting for me.

"You're such a strong swimmer. I can barely tread water." Seems she's accepted my suggestion to act as if I didn't just make her come. That'll make the rest of the trip smoother.

"I've seen you swim, you're not bad." My back against the pool's tiled wall, I stretch my arms along the edge. Casual. The opposite of how I'm feeling inside. "I can help you level up your skills when we get home. Teach you some strokes and techniques. You're going to be living at the house for a couple months, minimum. Might as well make the most of the time."

"That's what I'm hoping to do," she says, plastering herself to my chest, with her arms twined behind my neck. "I want you to teach me *all* the strokes and techniques."

"*Cricket.*" I grind her name out between clenched teeth. The concrete might actually crumble under my grip, I'm holding on that hard. Have to, otherwise, I'm going to touch her again. "This isn't how we pretend nothing happened on that lounge chair."

"That was your idea, not mine." Below the surface of the water, she wiggles until her legs are wrapped around my hips, a move that has her pussy cradling my steel-hard dick. "And for the record, it was a bad idea."

I laugh because she's cute, but there's nothing funny about my predicament. Or the blue balls I'm going to have. "You said you were embarrassed."

"Because I thought we'd be naked together, in a bed, in a dark room, the first time you made me come. I didn't expect to be so...front and center."

If she thinks she could be anything other than front and center around me, I did a decent job of hiding how I feel. Until today.

"Take me back to our room, I want to be naked with you," she says, nuzzling my neck with her cotton-candy-pink lips. "I know you want me, too."

No point in denying it, since there's a battering ram between my legs. "I can't fuck you, Cricket."

She pulls her head back, blinking at me with those big, blue eyes. "Do you—" Her eyelashes flutter as she whispers, "Do you have a disease?"

Bam, there it is. A one-way ticket out of her panties, forever. All I have to do is take it.

"No, I'm clean. I've never had anything." It's official, I'm a selfish bastard. I can tell myself I just didn't want her thinking less of me, and that's true, but not the whole truth. I want her more than I've ever wanted another woman. But I can't.

"Then why?" She frowns when I disentangle her from my body and swim out to a distance she can't reach.

Unlike my new bride, treading water is as easy as breathing for me. "You're Gina's best friend."

"Gina won't care. I think she'll be happy for us."

Fuck. I hadn't even considered the two of them discussing intimate, personal shit involving me. "Did you talk to Gina about—" My stomach rolls just thinking about the next words. "About the possibility of us getting together on this trip?"

"No..." She pulls her bottom lip between her teeth. "But, she shopped with me and watched me pack. She saw the bathing suits and dresses I brought."

"You're on vacation at an adults-only, Caribbean resort. Nothing wrong with wanting to attract the attention of some men your age while you're here. I'm sure that's all she thought."

"We're married, Troy. I would never cheat on you. Gina knows that."

"Gina knows we're married so you can get whatever medical attention you need. She wouldn't expect you to be faithful to me, and neither do I."

"But I don't want to be with anybody else." Her mouth curves into a frown, her eyelashes fluttering faster than butterfly wings. "Are you going to sleep with other women while we're married?"

Take the ticket, man. All I have to do is say yes, then she won't want to be with me. She'll probably hate me, but that doesn't matter. It might even be for the best. So, why is my head shaking? Fuck, I'm a stupid bastard.

"I won't be with anyone else while we're married." There. Committing to celibacy isn't the same as agreeing to fuck her. I'm good. This'll work.

"Okay."

The agreement's a little too easy, but this time, I

manage to keep my mouth closed. "I'm going to swim a few more laps."

"I'll be right here, admiring the view," she says, assuming my previous position with her arms stretched along the pool's edge. The water lifts her tits, as if putting them on display especially for me.

Talk about a view. I've always been a boob man, and Cricket's are spectacular. For now. If that lump turns out to be something serious… I shake my head to clear the negative thought. Whatever it is, we'll get through it. Whatever she needs, I'll make sure she gets it. I don't care what it costs or how long it takes.

"Come on, then," she says, letting her legs float up, smiling as she playfully kicks water in my direction. "Give *me* something to stare at."

Busted. And I can't help smiling right back at her. The urge to join her at the wall, pin her with my body and kiss her is so fucking strong. I can't give in again.

I wink instead, then fill my lungs and plunge beneath the water. To stay fit. To blow off some pent-up tension. But most of all, to give my gorgeous, temporary wife something to stare at.

four

CRICKET

IF THIS TRIP is a contest of wills, I'm going to win. But Troy's not making it easy.

After the single hottest moment of my life happened on that lounge chair yesterday, he spent the rest of the day—and night—putting us in public settings and safe situations. We ate lunch in the open-air buffet dining room, surrounded by dozens of other guests. The afternoon included a group sightseeing excursion. Dinner was in one of the smaller restaurants within the resort, but at a table in the middle of the room.

Behind the closed door of our room, he offered me first crack at the bathroom, then proceeded to fall asleep on the loveseat before I finished prepping for bed.

I stood beside him for a full two minutes, saying his name. I even poked him. He didn't budge. Didn't crack an eyelid. Didn't see me in the lingerie I'd chosen especially for this night. I silently conceded. Grudgingly swapped my negligee for boy shorts and a camisole, then spent my second night as a married woman *not* having sex with my hot husband.

This morning, I woke up to the *ping* of his incoming text, telling me to meet him in the lobby, and to wear comfortable pants. I'm not into working out, but I'd give it a fresh try for him, so I showed up in my best ass-high-lighting yoga pants and a sporty, cropped tank. My outfit had the desired effect. Troy didn't even try to keep his eyes off me. Unfortunately, he *did* keep his hands off me. All through our brief breakfast, and subsequent group activity —horseback riding. He didn't even boost me onto the saddle.

Wallowing and disappointment aside, it's actually a nice outing. The guide at the front of the line is entertaining, the other guests are friendly, and the jungle on either side of the path is pretty. The only negative is the distance from Troy. I can't even look back at him, because every time I ease up on the reins, my horse veers off course.

"You okay up there?" Troy calls when my horse makes another attempt to go left instead of forward.

I don't get the chance to answer. My horse does it for me—by ignoring my jerks and kicks, and walking into the greenery. To lie down.

"Oh my God, what are you doing?" Full panic mode engaged, I lean forward on the beast. "Please get up. *Please.*"

Troy's horse stops alongside, the model of good behavior. Holding the reins in one hand, Troy uses the other to give one of those loud, two-finger whistles. The rest of our group is far ahead, but the sound brings them to a stop, and the guide trots back to join us within seconds.

When nothing I try results in cooperation from the horse, I follow the guide's instructions and dismount. He does the same, then moves to my horse. He strokes its head, speaks to it gently, in a language I don't understand, finally coaxing it to stand.

"I'm not getting back on that horse."

"No, she is too tired to carry a rider, even one as small as you. We are close to the end, I'll lead her back." The guide nods at his horse. "You can ride with me."

"She'll ride with me," Troy says before I can respond. There's a no-tolerance edge to his deep voice, matched by the hard set of his handsome, strong jaw as he dismounts. "I'm an experienced rider and my horse is big enough to carry us both. Our combined weight won't put too much strain on him for a short distance."

The guide doesn't argue, just watches closely while Troy boosts me onto the saddle. "Take it slow. I'm leading the rest of the group back to the ranch. Stay on the trail, and we'll meet you there."

"We're good." Troy dismisses the guide with those two words. Within a minute, the guide, my horse, and the rest of our group are all out of sight.

We're alone. Crammed into a saddle, my back to his chest. My ass to his cock, growing thick and hard against my lower back. We couldn't get physically closer without being sexually interlocked.

"You know, I was kind of bummed about this horseback riding thing, but it's, um, growing on me."

"Yeah, it is." His gruff laugh against my ear sends a ripple of awareness straight to my clit. "Sorry about that."

"You have nothing to be sorry about," I say, wiggling against him. "Honestly, I couldn't have planned today any better."

"It's the opposite of what I planned." His muscular legs

squeeze briefly, then, like magic, we're moving. No kicking or rein snapping required.

"If you didn't want to be this close to me, you should have let me ride with the guide."

"You're right, I probably should have."

"Then why didn't you?" I know the answer, but I want to hear him say it.

"I don't want anyone else touching you. I tell myself I'll be okay with it, that it's what's best for you. But the thought of it makes me fucking crazy. Having self-control around you is getting harder by the minute."

"I can feel that. And I like it."

Another deep rumble slides into my ear. "The island is bringing out the bad girl in you."

"*Woman.* You need to stop thinking of me as a girl."

"I never have. Even when I met you. Felt like a dirty old man, but I couldn't stop myself. Still can't."

Finally, everything I've ever wanted to hear. Well, almost everything. "You've never been a dirty old man. You were thirty-four when we met, and I was eighteen. We've always been consenting adults." When all I get is silence, I move my hands from the saddle horn to his quadriceps. "We're *married* consenting adults now. You don't need self-control with me. I want you, Troy. Just as much as you want me."

"Not possible."

The admission fuels my confidence. My boldness. "Then fuck me tonight."

"Can't."

Not the answer I want. Or need. Now that I'm not holding the saddle, each stride of our rhythmic ride pushes my clit against the horn. Again and again, like a vibrator on the slowest, most agonizingly teasing setting. I pretend to shift for comfort, but it's to get more pressure. Not enough. I need more, and I need it from him.

"Please," I say, taking one of his hands from the reins, and placing it between my legs.

"Fuck. How am I supposed to resist you?" He slides his hand inside my pants. A tortured groan vibrates against me when his fingers reach my pussy. "You're so fucking wet."

"Because of you." I moan as he works my clit, barely breathing as he pushes me closer and closer to the edge.

"I wish I was eating your sweet little pussy right now."

The words, the thought of his face between my legs, tips me over. "Yes, God, *Troy...*"

He curses a string of perfect, filthy endearments as I come against his hand for what feels like forever, and also like a blink that ends too soon.

"I have to know." The spandex snaps against my waist, then he sucks his fingers into his mouth. "Fuck, so good." He nuzzles his face against my hair, until his mouth is against my ear. "Hold your pants open so I can have another taste."

I don't have to ask if he's serious, I know he is. And I love it. I pull the stretchy fabric forward as far as the saddle allows.

"You don't know what you do to me," he says, slipping his fingers between my legs, sliding and rolling them across my sensitive flesh, then sucking them into his mouth again. "I'm fucking addicted."

"Good thing I've got an endless supply of what you need."

"Good thing." His deep, rumbling chuckle fills my head as the trail opens into the ranch. He smooths my pants into place, then takes proper hold of the reins.

"Thanks for the ride," I say, tipping my head to smile up at him.

"My pleasure." He doesn't say any of the other words I'd like to hear. Just presses a kiss to my temple and steers us toward the barn.

But the day's not over. And neither are we.

TROY

On short notice, I could only swing a week off from work. I took what I could get, because giving Cricket this vacation was important. Not only to keep up the appearance that our marriage is legit. Because she's going to have a lot of heavy shit to deal with once we're back home.

I wanted her to have a chance to let loose. Hook up with someone who'd appreciate her and show her a good time, in and out of bed, before her world—and gorgeous body— might change forever. I thought I could step aside, hide out for a few days. Distance myself while she got wild with someone.

I didn't plan to *be* the someone. I tried not to be. But now that I've kissed her, touched her... Now that I've tasted her...

I throw back the remaining rum in my glass, then set the empty on the balcony table. That's my second since we got back from our day's activities. The booze isn't helping me forget my favorite activity of all—making Cricket come. I want to do it again. To bury my face between her legs and eat that sweet pussy all night long. To sink my perpetually rock-hard dick into her hot body.

I can't do either of those things. I know that. Just not sure where I'm going to find the restraint.

"Troy?" Her voice drifts through the screen, from inside the suite.

"Out here." It's not really *safe* on the balcony—no place is safe when I'm with her. I proved that at the pool yesterday, and on the back of a horse today. But the first-floor balcony, with its glass railing and courtyard view, is the safest I can get right now. Somehow, I have to stay clear of that bed. For two more nights.

"I'm ready," she says, sliding the door open, and stepping out in a red dress that hugs her curves, shows off her tits, and screams sex. "Are you ready?"

So fucking ready. "Yeah." No point suggesting she go without me. Tried it during dinner and got shut down. If I don't take her to the resort's nightclub, we're spending the evening in our room together. We'll be safer on the dancefloor.

I push up from the chair, making no attempt to hide the fact that I'm checking her out. "You look incredible."

"Good enough to eat?" she asks, batting her eyelashes at me. "And fuck?"

"Definitely." I move in closer, grinning when I hear her suck in a breath. "But it's not going to happen. Not unless you changed your mind about picking someone up."

Her angry kitten noise makes me laugh—until she adds some verbal claws. "And if I decide to bring some random guy back here and bang him, where will you sleep?"

I know she's taunting me. Waving a hypothetical red flag in hopes that I'll charge. Nope. Not throwing fuel on the fire. Things are hot enough between us already.

"On a lounge chair." I nod toward the courtyard below. "Close enough to come to your rescue if you call me. Far enough away to give you privacy."

"You've really thought about this." Her pretty lips form a frown. "You actually *want* me to hook up with somebody else."

Yet another opportunity to extract myself from the mess I've made so far. But I'm still too selfish to pull the trigger. "I want this to be an amazing vacation for you. One with no regrets, and lots of exciting, positive memories to look back on."

"Good." She loops her arm beneath mine and tugs me toward the door. "Let's go make some."

I laugh and let her pull me into the suite, then out to the hall, and through the perfect, Caribbean night, to the resort's nightclub. It's not exactly booming at nine thirty, but there are enough people to make it natural.

She stops near the bar, meets my gaze without looking up, because the heels she's wearing put us nearly eye to eye. "I just realized, I've never seen you dance."

If I do the math, it's been close to a decade. I quit clubbing around the time Cricket hit puberty. She would've been realizing she liked boys, while I was winding down my party profile. Hell of a difference. More proof that I'm too old for her.

"It's been a while."

"Are you going to step on my feet?" she asks, placing a palm against my chest.

"Only if you want me to."

"If only you were that agreeable to my other suggestions." She gives me a playful nudge, then grabs my hand and squeezes as the music changes. "Oh, I love this song."

"Then, let's go carve up the dance floor."

By the time we reach the growing group of bouncing bodies, she's beaming brighter than the kaleidoscope of spotlights. She's happy. Excited. Making those positive memories I want her to have. With me.

I'd be lying if I said I only care that she's happy, not how she gets there. Truth is, I love being the man she's happy with. Making her smile is everything. I don't want it to end when we leave the dance floor. I don't want it to end at the bedroom door.

For better or worse, I'm going to give her whatever she wants tonight.

We reach a pocket of free space, and I twirl her under my arm, smiling like a monkey when she laughs as if she's having the time of her life. I fucking love that sound.

My hands find her waist, and I tug her against me. "Time to show me your moves, Mrs. Mannington."

Her eyes light up and she wraps her arms around my neck. Calling her that is a mistake. The first of many I'll make tonight, no doubt. And I'm going to enjoy every damn one.

TROY

"Well, how'd the old man stack up?" I ask, as we roll out of the club, energized and sweaty from two solid hours of bumping and grinding. I'm not fishing for compliments. I'm reminding her that I'm thirty-nine, not twenty-three. A last-ditch effort to push her away. A lame one, but it's all I've got left.

She practically throws herself at me, plastering her wicked-hot body against my chest, as she has at least a dozen times tonight. "Oh my God, you were amazing. I had so much fun with you." No acknowledgment of the *old* comment. Maybe she didn't hear it. Maybe she truly doesn't care.

At the moment, neither do I. "You want to come back tomorrow night?"

"Yes!" she squeals, literally, while bouncing up and down. "I wish we had more time here."

"Me too." I wish time would stand still, and we could live in this window forever. Together, without judgment. Without health concerns looming in the wings. Those are next week's problems. "Want to grab a moonlight swim before going back to the room?"

"Before?" Little wrinkles form when she scrunches her nose. How she's adorable and sexy at the same time is a mystery, but she is. "What about swimsuits?"

"What about them?"

Her eyes open wide as it hits her, then narrow, just as fast. "Wait a minute. Are you going in with me, or is this another tease?" She gasps as I palm her ass, and pull her tight against the never-ending hard-on she inspires.

"No more teasing. The swim, and afterward. Whatever you want from me, you'll get."

"Even if I want everything?"

"Yeah, sweetheart." I slide my hand to her nape. Thread my fingers through her hair, and look into her beautiful eyes. "I can't say no to you anymore. I don't want to." I seal my mouth against hers, groaning at the taste of her lips, at her tongue dancing with mine. Even better than the first time, at our wedding. I was fucking crazy avoiding this. Two days I could've been kissing her, wasted. No more. Not one more wasted minute.

"Wow," she whispers when we break to catch our breath. "That was...wow."

"That was the beginning, sweetheart. When you close your eyes for sleep tonight, you're going to have a new definition of 'wow.'"

"Maybe we should skip the swim, and go straight to our room."

My lips brush hers as I shake my head. "We have two more days in paradise, and I want to fill them with as many memories as possible."

"God, finally," she says, smiling against my mouth. She shrieks when I scoop her off her feet, into my arms. Her head falls back as I move, her joyous laughter rising into the warm night air like the sweetest music I've ever heard.

I want to hear it all night long. Every night, every day. For the rest of my life.

Fuck me, I'm in love with her.

CRICKET

WHEN TROY SUGGESTED A SWIM, I thought he meant in the pool. Then he carried me past it. The beach is empty, except for us and whatever creatures are awake beneath the ocean's dark surface. I'd be scared if I were alone. If I were doing this with anybody other than Troy. I know he'll take care of me. He has since I met him, in little ways that would fill a book if I listed them all, and enormous ways, like marrying me. I trust him more than anyone.

Seeing the moonlight bounce off the Caribbean, hearing the waves lightly lapping the shore as he crouches before me, unbuckling my strappy heels...the beach is so much better than the pool. Even though it's late, the sand is still warm beneath my bare feet as he sets each on the ground.

"We don't have towels," I say, as he unties the laces of his Oxfords.

"You can use my shirt."

I try not to drool as he stands, unbuttons the aforementioned white dress shirt, then shrugs it off his muscular torso. "I might not give it back, you know."

He moves behind me, his chuckle raising goosebumps on my skin as he lowers the zipper of my dress. "That's okay." His fingers loop under the spaghetti straps, then draw them over my shoulders, and down my arms. "You're going to give me stuff I'm definitely keeping."

Please, let him mean my heart.

"Fuck, you're beautiful," he says, circling back to face me, his hand never disconnecting from my skin for a moment.

Every part of me heats beneath his gaze, his touch. When he steps closer and cups my face in his warm, strong hands, my heartbeat is louder than the ocean's waves.

"The most beautiful woman I've ever seen."

My hands find his buckle as he kisses me. I fight the urge to pull him against me, working his belt and zipper open instead, then pushing his khakis down.

He groans into my mouth as I palm his cock through the underwear. Steps back when I try to peel them off. His white boxer briefs practically glow in the dark, and there's no mistaking the sizeable bulge he's packing up front. "Not here."

"But...I thought we were going skinny-dipping," I say when he takes my hand and leads me toward the ocean.

"Must've been wishful thinking, because all I said was 'moonlight swim.'"

"You also said 'no more teasing.'" I sound like a pouting child, not the woman I want him to see me as.

"And I meant it." He draws me into the water, pulling me against him when we get waist-deep. "I'm going to make you come tonight, as many times and ways as you want. You want my fingers in your pussy? I'll give you that here and now. You want me to eat your sweet little pussy, fill you with my dick? Those things are going to wait until we're in our room. I've ached for you for five long years, Cricket. I tried to fight it, deny it, resist you. It's the only goal I've ever set and failed to achieve. I want you too fucking much. Now that I get to have you, I'm taking my time. In private. I'm going to lay you out properly. Worship every inch of you."

"God, yes." I twine my arms behind his neck, wrap my legs around his waist. "You're not the only one who's been waiting forever for this night."

He takes us into deeper water, groaning as I rock and rub myself against his hard length. "There's one more thing you should know before you let me into your sexy body." His hand tangles in my hair, tipping my head back to meet his heated, hungry gaze. "I'm not just making you come all night. I'm kissing, touching, licking, and fucking you until I *ruin* you. I'm going to make sure your body sings my name every time you come, for the rest of your life. No matter who's inside you, you're going to think of me."

"Only you." Water slaps at our backs as I grind on him, harder and faster, until I'm so close to the edge, my vision blurs. "There's only ever going to be you."

His growl fills my mouth as he kisses me hard. His fingertips curl into my butt, and he drives me up and down against his cock, the meaty tip hitting my clit exactly right until I come. He holds me tight as the ripples subside, stroking my back and kissing my shoulder.

"Take me to our room and ruin me," I say, once I can breathe again.

His deep, sexy chuckle slides into my ear, the promise of more coming to come.

TROY

I might burn in hell for what I'm about to do. For the stuff I've already done. Too damn bad. Let the chips fall, because I sure have. I know I'll have to let her go once we're back home. Not tonight. Tonight's about getting as close as she'll let me.

She protested when I sent her to shower alone. There's no way I could have been naked with her and not fucked her. And I will fuck her in the shower. Definitely. That's not how the first time's going down, though. Because I need a lot more space for *going down*.

Feels like my dick has been perpetually hard for days. Not for lack of beating off, I've done that five fucking times since we got to the resort. The last time was only a few hours ago, before we went dancing. It barely took the edge off. Only one thing will satisfy the hunger I've been fighting. Tonight, I'm going to feast.

My dick's at full mast when I open the bathroom door. I don't bother to cover up. Nuance unrequired. I don't need one more thing to take off.

Or so I thought.

"Jesus fuck," I say, at the sight of Cricket on the bed, looking like a goddess in a pink bra that pushes her perfect tits to the overflow level, and panties that are barely more than a collection of strings. Taking those off is going to be a pleasure.

A couple of strides and I'm on the bed, caging her beneath me. "You're so beautiful."

"I know you like me in pink."

"Right now, I'll like you *out of* pink." I dip down for a taste of her shiny lips, unhooking the front clasp of her bra and palming one glorious tit. I pull back when she gasps into my mouth. "Did I hurt you? Fuck, I didn't think about the lump."

Her golden hair shimmers against the duvet as she shakes her head. "The lump is in the other one."

"I'll try to be gentle."

"I don't need you to be gentle, touching it doesn't hurt."

"I'll try anyway."

"*Don't.* Please, Troy." She cups my face, strokes my brow line, currently bunched and tense. "I don't know what's going to happen to my body when we get home. I need you to just...be real with me. Rough, hard, or gentle. I want it all with you. While I'm still normal."

"You could never be normal. You're amazing."

"For now," she whispers, her hands sliding from my face.

It's time for me to show up. Really show up. I shift to my knees, bracketing her hips between my legs, and look down at her. "For always. Your body is hot as fuck, but you're so much more than your sexy tits and curves. You're determined and smart, but you're also calm and kind, and fun to be around, no matter what we're doing. You're an incredible woman, Cricket. The inside as much as outside."

"Thank you."

"It's all true." So are the things I didn't say. Like, how I'm not just impressed by her, I'm fucking in love with her.

She reaches for my dick, still standing at the ready. "Then, how about you use *this* damn impressive thing to get better acquainted with my *inside*."

I groan at the sight of her holding my cock. Deciding to fuck Cricket definitely makes me a selfish son of a bitch, but I'm not selfish enough to do it without making her come first. Or, maybe that makes me *more* selfish. Either way, putting my dick in her sweet body isn't happening yet. Not until I put my tongue there.

I drop to my forearms and plunder her mouth. She tastes like fresh, sweet heaven, and fuck me, I can't get enough. My dick is hard as steel, and I press it against its future home, rocking my hips as if I'm fucking her. Soon. It has to be soon.

She wraps her legs around me, her heels spurring me close with each thrust. "God, when are you going to stop teasing and fuck me?"

"Not teasing you. Getting you ready for me."

"I've been ready for you for five years," she says, dragging her nails down my back, to my naked butt. "Don't make me wait anymore. I want you inside me."

"I want that too. But I'm a greedy bastard, and I want to taste you first." I nip her bottom lip, then soothe it with my tongue before moving downward. Her neck gets the same treatment, each nip eliciting a gasp that's a sexy mixture of surprise, pain, and pleasure.

"Are you going to leave a mark?" she asks after my soothing lick becomes a suck.

"No, I don't want you to be embarrassed."

"I wouldn't be. Actually, I'd like it if people looked at me and saw your hickeys and bitemarks on me." She pulls her bottom lip between her teeth while sliding her fingers through my hair. "Will you give me some? Please?"

Thirty-nine-year-old men don't give hickeys. Sure as fuck not intentionally. But that's exactly what I'm going to do, because I'm way past saying no to her.

"Anywhere I want?" I ask, tracing her collarbone with my tongue.

"Yes." Her whisper becomes a gasp when I nip the spot where her shoulder curves into the column of her neck.

I suck her soft skin between my lips, between my teeth, long and hard. I release the pressure and ease back to survey my work. "That's one."

Her beautiful eyes open wide. "Really? You gave me a hickey?"

"Oh, yeah." Now that I see it, I like it. Every man in the resort is going to know she belongs to someone. And since I don't plan to leave her side for the rest of the trip, they'll know that someone is me. "You have more skimpy bikinis to taunt me with?"

"A few." She giggles. "Why?"

"You'll see," I say, moving lower. The upper swell of her full tits is my next target. I choose a spot and get to work, then place a gentle kiss on the mark I've left. "That's two."

She lifts her head, her face beaming with a wide smile when she looks down at the coin-sized strawberry. "Oh my God, it's so dark."

"It's a bruise."

"A love bruise." A deep-pink blush floods her cheeks. "I'm not saying you love me. You know what I mean, right?"

The perfect opportunity to tell her exactly how I feel is right here, on a silver platter. But I don't. "I do," I say, instead.

"Give me more." Her eyes shine, and her tits jiggle as she wiggles her sexy body. "I want everyone to know where you've been."

"Dirty girl."

"When I'm with you," she says, holding my gaze.

Fuck, I want that to be always. I'll settle for a couple of fantastic days. I pepper her beautiful body with more *love bruises*. A couple more on her tits, one above the swell of her pussy. People are going to look at her, then look at me, and think I'm a dirty old bastard. And I can't fucking wait.

"Time for these to go." I slide the minuscule panties down and off, then reposition, pushing her legs apart and kneeling between them. A man at the altar of perfect fucking pussy. I could worship here for the rest of my life.

I run my hands all over her skin. Soft touches, firm squeezes. Every inch gets kisses, licks, and nips while I watch her expressions and actions, listen to her sounds. Learning her secrets, everything she likes, what makes her arch closer, desperate for more.

She moans when I suck her nipple into my mouth, laving, nibbling, sucking. "Oh, God, bite me harder."

I growl and pull her nipple between my teeth. Harder than before, hard enough to make a sharp gasp rise from her parted lips. I slide one hand between her legs, groaning at the slick heat that welcomes my fingers.

"Troy..." She breathes my name like a plea, as I roll circles around her clit. "I need to come."

"I'll take care of you, sweetheart. Going to make you come all night long." I shift to the other tit, giving it the same attention while I rub her clit the way I know she likes. I move back and forth, filling my mouth with one perfect tit, then the other. Sucking and biting, until both nipples are bullet-hard peaks.

Her breath hitches, her hips rising to meet my hand in jerky, desperate thrusts. The sexiest moan fills the air as she rides the orgasm until there's nothing left but shaking thighs and an irresistible, breathy giggle.

"Fuck, you're beautiful when you come. Need to taste it this time."

Her eyes open wide. So do her legs, as I kiss my way down her body and settle in for the feast I've been craving since I met her. "How many times are you going to make me come?"

"As many as I can wring out of your sexy body." I hold her gaze while placing a kiss on the silky skin above the hood of her clit. My plan to watch her disappears the instant my tongue connects with her pussy. Can't keep my eyes open while I'm in fucking heaven.

I band my arms around her thighs and lick her, top to bottom, growling against her skin. I'm already addicted to her fresh, tangy essence. I burrow in, eating her hot little pussy like a starving man. I need her sweet cream all over my face. Need her to come undone. To beg me for more. To tell me she can't take more, all at the same time.

"Troy," she says, pushing her fingers through my hair, those pretty, painted nails of hers raking the scalp beneath. She's close. Ready. Needy.

Part of me wants to back off. Keep her on the edge so I can stay right where I am. Because, fuck, I don't want this to end. I also want inside her. I want it all.

I slip one hand between her legs, groan as I slide a single finger into her pussy. Fuck, so hot. So tight. I give her two fingers, growling when her hips come off the bed and her legs open wider.

"More," she says, her breathy voice becoming a moan as I add a third. "Troy..."

My body's on autopilot, humping the mattress as I

finger-fuck her tight little pussy. No more drawing it out, I need her to come. I suck her clit, circle, and flick it with my tongue, until she's bucking against my mouth, her sexy moans filling the room.

I ease back when her moans turn to giggles. "So fucking sexy." I place a kiss on either side of her pussy, then crawl up her body and claim her beautiful mouth.

She moans and folds her arms and legs around me, pulling me onto her. "Fuck me now," she says, as we kiss. "No more waiting."

"Condom." I get the word out, but the head of my dick is already cradled between her slick pussy lips.

"I'm on the Pill, and I'm clean, I promise."

Fuck, *she's* promising *me*? I don't deserve her. But I'm sure as fuck going to take her. "I'm clean too," I say, pushing deeper. Just the tip, but fuck, she feels so good. "I swear I'd never do anything that'd hurt you."

"I know, I trust you."

Fuck, she's everything. *Every. Fucking. Thing.* I crush my lips against hers before I tell her that, in three short words. I rock my hips, groaning at the sensation. The slick heat. I'm barely inside her, just a couple of inches, and I'm already on fire with the need to come.

Her heels spur my butt, urging me closer.

"Tell me if it's too much," I say when she gasps as I push deeper.

"It'll never be too much with you. Give me everything."

"You have every part of me, sweetheart. Everything I have is only for you." It's as close as I let myself get to telling her. I slide all the way home, groaning at the squeeze around my dick. "You're so fucking beautiful. So perfect."

Her breath catches as I bury myself completely, balls-deep in her pussy. "You're so big."

"You made me this way. Now I'm going to fuck you deep and hard, and you're going to come all over this big dick."

She moans when I thrust inside again. Digs her nails into my shoulders when I roll my hips to grind against her clit. "Don't stop," she says, as I slide back.

I chuckle and nip her neck, then lick the spot while filling her pussy again. "You know I'm going to make you come. But you're so fucking tight, I won't last once you're squeezing me with your sweet pussy, and I need to fuck you hard before that happens."

"God, yes. Fuck me hard. Fuck me any way you want."

Fire rages in my balls at the thought of doing *everything* I want. "Careful what you offer, or I just might fuck every part of you."

"Do it," she says, licking her lips as my next hard thrust pushes her higher up the bed. "Make all of me yours."

The beast in me roars. I pull out, roll her over, and position the head of my dick against her tight little pucker. "Ever had a dick in this sexy ass?"

"No," she whispers. "But I want yours there."

"Fuck." I press against her rim, just the tiniest bit. So fucking tempting, but she's not ready for this. I reposition my cock, grab her hips, and thrust into her pussy, fast and hard.

She moans as I seat myself deep. Her breath hitches as I spread her cheeks and press the tip of my spit-moistened finger against her pucker.

"You like that?" I ask, rolling it until the smallest bit slips inside.

"Yes." She's almost breathless, and I've barely breached her.

"Easy, baby." I add a healthy dose of saliva and push

deeper, banding my arm around her and holding her in place when her body instinctively jerks forward. "This is just the tip of one finger. You're going to need to take a lot more before I can fuck you. One finger, then two, then three."

"*Three?*" Her voice is a whispered squeak.

"Oh, yeah. My dick's thicker than three fingers." I pull back and thrust into her pussy again, making her moan. "Feel how big it is?"

"*Yes.*"

"You sure you want that big, hard dick fucking your ass?"

"Yes," she says, panting as I work my finger to the middle knuckle while fucking her pussy. "I want everything with you."

I get my finger good and slick, then ease it into her ass again, all the way this time. "You're fucking perfect," I say, finger-fucking her ass and pumping her pussy until stars roll up behind my eyes. "Need to feel you come." I slide my other hand between her legs, rubbing her clit hard and fast. "You own this dick. Come all over it, milk me dry." I grit my teeth, I'm holding on by a thread, but I will hold on, as long as it takes for her to—

"*Troy...*" Her body jerks beneath mine. Her ragged moans fill the room, my head, my fucking heart, as she rides my hand. Squeezes my dick, my finger.

I unload like a geyser, rutting on my sexy-as-fuck wife like a wild beast in mating season.

My wife. Mating season. I never gave having more kids a single thought until this moment, but with Cricket, it's crystal clear. I'd give her a baby if she wanted. I'd give her anything. All she'd have to do is ask.

Which she won't, because she's twenty-three. She's studying her ass off to start a career, not be the stay-home-and-raise-babies wife of a man old enough to be *her* father. No matter how interested she is right now, how hot our physical connection is, this time we're sharing is temporary. Our marriage is a stopover in her life, not the final destination.

I need to remember that. Enjoy the moment and keep my feelings locked down, so we can be friends, once her medical stuff—and our marriage—is in her rearview.

"Wow," she says, as I slide free of her body and roll us onto our sides.

"Exactly what I was thinking." It's a lie as fat as my dick was a few minutes ago. I bury my face in her hair and breathe her in. "More 'wow' coming your way soon."

"More?"

I chuckle and press a kiss to her head, then slide my hand to her tit and strum her nipple. "Oh yeah. Did you forget what I promised to do to you tonight?"

"You said you're going to worship me."

"That's right, and I've only started with that." I pull her closer, so my dick is nestled between our bodies. "What else did I say I'm going to do?"

"Ruin me," she whispers.

"That's right." Goosebumps rise beneath my fingertips as I trail them downward, to the pussy I know I'll never get enough of. "And I'm a man of my word."

"That's one of the things I love about you."

I freeze, mid-stroke, at her words. I can't see her face, but beneath my arm, her heart is beating like one of the dance anthems from the club tonight.

"I didn't mean to freak you out," she says.

"Not freaked out at all."

"Okay." A nervous laugh rises from lips I can't see. "You just went all stiff on me when I said the L-word. Not the good kind of stiff."

It's the perfect segue, and I'm smart enough to take it. "You ready for more of the good kind of stiff?"

"Already?" She twists to look over her shoulder, her eyes opening wide when I slide my thickening cock between her thighs. "Did you take a Viagra?"

I shake my head while rolling her clit between my fingers. "It's you. It's always you, Cricket."

She wriggles, turning to face me. Our gazes lock as she wraps her arms around my neck, and drapes one leg over my hip. "And it's always only you for me."

There's a shift. Something big, almost tangible. As if everything I want is right there, in front of me, and all I have to do is stake a claim, and it'll be mine. I'm tempted. So fucking tempted.

When I open my mouth, I choke. Chicken out, and kiss her instead. Then cup her ass and slide into her hot, welcoming body. Nice and deep, but slow, this time. Long thrusts with lots of lingering grinding against her clit. I kiss her as if this is the only chance I'll ever get, making love to her mouth while I fuck her the same way. I won't say the words, but I'm going to make damn sure she *feels* how much I love her.

Her breath hitches mid-kiss. She's right there, on the edge, and I'm going to give her everything she needs.

I cup her ass and pull her as close as two bodies can get. I mold my hand to her nape, holding her to our kiss while I rock my pelvis against her clit.

Her soft moan fills my mouth as her body jerks and trembles against mine. Her sweet pussy clenches around my dick, and I push deeper, groaning as I follow her over, again.

When she goes pliant in my arms, I keep kissing her. Softer kisses, but still deep. Even when she giggles against my lips, I don't stop. I don't let her escape. I'm not ready to let go. Who the fuck am I kidding—I never will be.

six

CRICKET

THE ROOM IS FULLY LIT with sunshine when I open my eyes. I'm alone in bed, but this morning is different from its predecessors because I didn't sleep solo last night. Troy's pillow is empty now, but his handsome head was there all night long. Well, after he finished putting it in more interesting places, like between my legs. Which he did four times.

That's more oral than I've received in the past year—in one night. Four glorious, body-shaking orgasms delivered by the man who's inspired me to masturbate more times than I can count. I may have missed the odd day here and there—because, lady reasons—but other than that, he's been the only man in my head. Even when I've had boyfriends. I tried thinking of them, but my mind always strayed back to Troy.

Yes, it was only mental cheating, but I broke up with those guys. Not only because of imaginary indiscretions. Being with anyone other than Troy, in or out of the bedroom, in or out of reality, never felt right. I was meant for one man only. Holy crap, was he worth the wait.

I roll toward the empty pillow, my pulse rising when I spot a note. I reach for it, my engagement ring sparkling in the sunlight, and I have to stop and admire it for the hundredth time.

Troy didn't have to buy me a ring. He *absolutely* didn't have to buy me a beautiful, full-carat, princess-cut diamond that cost more than I make in two months. He has worked hard to forge a successful career, and he's financially comfortable, but he's not filthy rich. He can shrug the ring off as no big deal all he wants, but I know otherwise. This ring is more than a showpiece to make people believe we're in love. It's the silent, shiny truth.

Last night was more than hours of intensely hot sex. It was the not-so-silent, sweaty truth. Everything he does shows me how he feels about me. If only he would say the words, too.

I pluck the note from his pillow. Troy's strong printing commands the interior of the folded paper, and I can't help smiling at the first word I see—sweetheart.

SWEETHEART, YOU ARE SO FUCKING GORGEOUS, LYING THERE WITH YOUR HAIR MESSED UP FROM ALL OUR FUCKING, AND YOUR PRETTY LIPS PUFFY FROM ALL OUR KISSING. I'M SO TEMPTED TO SKIP THE GYM AND CRAWL BACK INTO BED WITH YOU. TO CAREFULLY PULL THE SHEET BACK AND WAKE YOU BY KISSING EVERY INCH OF YOUR SEXY BODY BEFORE I SLIDE INSIDE YOU. I'M ADDICTED TO YOU, MRS. MANNINGTON. SLEEP WELL, BEAUTY. YOU'RE GOING TO NEED IT.

My happy squeal breaks the silence in our honeymoon suite. I'll never be able to stop loving this man. I'll never want to.

CRICKET

The resort's gym isn't busy when I walk in. No big shock to me, vacations and heavy lifting don't go together in my book. But Troy never misses a day. Since that dedication has given him the wicked body I enjoy ogling, I'm not about to suggest he change his routine. Even if it did deprive me of wake-up sex.

I'm not dressed for exercise, and I feel out of place weaving around the array of machines, benches, and racks. That feeling amplifies when I spot Troy sitting on an incline bench, smiling and chatting with an attractive, fit woman.

His gaze shifts to meet mine, his eyebrows pulling together as I force myself to smile. He can tell I'm faking. He knows me inside and out, now more than ever.

I know Troy pretty damn well, too. And I plan to make sure no other woman gets the same opportunity.

Spandex-chick follows Troy's gaze, her expression dropping at the sight of me headed their way.

"Hi, honey," I say, stepping between Troy's legs, and pressing my body against his chest. "I missed you in bed this morning."

He chuckles and palms my ass. "Did you see my note?"

"I did." I flick my hair over my shoulder, a move that makes two of last night's hickeys visible. The weight of the woman's stare raises my temperature several degrees. Just in case there's any doubt in her mind, I run my fingers through Troy's hair and leave my hand at the base of his neck. "Don't be so considerate tomorrow. I'd rather you wake me up the way you said than get another hour's sleep."

"Noted. I'm almost done in here. A couple more sets, then I'll meet you back in the room, and grab a shower."

"I'll wash your back...and your front." It's brazen talk in front of a complete stranger, but I can't seem to stop. It also does the trick, because the woman lifts one hand in a surrendering wave, then disappears. "That's right," I say, under my breath. "Get away from my man."

His eyebrows rise as a laugh slides through his smiling lips. "You're jealous."

"Of course, I am. She was pretty, with a nice body, and—"

"And she's not you," he says, tugging me closer. "I promised there'd only be you, and I won't break that promise."

"Even if you want to," I whisper.

"I don't." He cups my jaw in one strong hand, his gaze searing me with its intensity. "You're the woman I want to be with. Did I not make that clear last night?"

Every cell in my body is awake and on fire now. "Yes, but...maybe you should remind me anyway."

"Not maybe. Definitely." The smack he delivers to my butt rings in the mostly empty room, then he rises from the bench. "I'm done here."

"I thought you had more sets to do?"

"I'll finish my workout in our room." His wink sends my pulse racing. The muscles in his broad back, chest, and strong arms flex as he wipes down the equipment he used. "Be right back," he says, before striding to the locker room.

I glance around the gym, fleetingly meeting the attentive—and disapproving—gazes of several patrons. I fluff my hair into place over the front of my shoulder to cover the hickeys, then stare at my feet until Troy returns.

"What's wrong?" he asks, tilting my chin upward.

"People were..." I shake my head.

"People were what?"

"It's nothing. I'm being oversensitive."

His jaw clenches, his gaze darting around the room before returning to my face. "If anyone did or said something to you, I need to know." Protecting me, as always, in whatever way is necessary.

"There's nothing to tell. Nobody has come near me. They were just...looking. And that's my fault because I marched in here and made a spectacle because I was jealous of a woman talking to you. It was immature and uncalled for, and I'm sorry if I embarrassed you."

"I don't embarrass easily."

My cheeks heat at the memory of Troy standing in the doorway of his living room, wearing nothing more than a pair of snug-fitting, crowded boxer briefs, knowing fully well I was gawking at every hard inch of him. He definitely doesn't embarrass easily.

He strokes my jawline, cradling my face in one strong palm. "I understand how you felt when you saw us talking. Watching an endless stream of guys talk to you over the last five years has almost killed me." It's not the full admission I'm desperate for him to finally make, but it's close enough for now.

"I think we should go back to the room and make up for all that lost time."

60

His laugh booms in the open space, drawing judgmental stares from everyone in the place, once again. He doesn't spare a glance for any of them. All of his attention remains on me. "There aren't enough hours in the day, or days in the year for us to catch up. But we can make damn sure we don't lose another minute."

"I love that idea." And him. God, I love him. The untake-backable words hang in the back of my throat, threatening to leap from my lips if I open them again. I smile instead, sending up a little prayer when he takes my hand and squeezes it.

"For the record," he says, leading me out, still oblivious —or simply unconcerned—about the gawking stares tracking our departure. "Even though you'll never have a reason to be jealous, I like that you were. Guess that's my arrogant caveman coming out."

"Can we get him an animal-print loincloth? Because he'd look super-hot in one."

"Whatever you want," he says, laughing and dropping one hand to the small of my back while guiding me through the doorway. "But if you get to dress me up, I get a turn with you."

"Deal."

"You're boldly agreeable for a woman who doesn't know the inner-workings of my filthy mind and all its fantasies about you." Not just fantasies, fantasies about *me*.

"It sounds as if you're trying to spook me, but maybe it's you who should be scared."

"Yeah?" He puts an arm around my shoulders and grins down at me, as we make our way across the resort grounds. "Hit me with your dirtiest fantasy. I guarantee it won't be too much for me to handle."

"You sound boldly confident for a man who doesn't

know the inner-workings of *my* filthy mind, and all the late-night, masturbatory fantasies I've had about *you*."

A deep groan rumbles its way up from his chest. "Fuck. Just added a new fantasy to my list."

"What is it?" I know what the answer will be, but I want to hear him say it. I am his dirty girl, after all.

"Going to need to watch you getting yourself off to one of your fantasies." He slides his hand up my shoulder, then into the front of my sundress, to my breast. "Yeah, that's going to be your first orgasm when we get back to the room."

A shiver ripples through me, and it's not solely from Troy's fingers toying with my nipple. He has no idea how closely his wish intersects with my fantasy. "Okay. And what do I get?"

"Anything you want."

"Be careful what you offer," I say, mimicking his words from last night. "I might ask for everything."

He tugs me closer as we walk, pressing a kiss to my temple. "Ask away, sweetheart."

If I don't lose my nerve, I just might.

TROY

The suite is cloaked in semi-darkness when I step out of the bathroom. Cricket has drawn the curtains, but there's enough light to see her lying on the bed. By the time I reach it, my eyes have fully adjusted, and I can make out every sexy detail.

Her white camisole is pushed up above her tits. She's playing with one, tugging at the nipple. A pair of white panties lay beside her hip, and her hand is between her legs, stroking that pretty pussy of mine.

And it is mine. For now.

I get my wish about watching, but it's on her terms. Because, apparently, having me catch her masturbating is *her* fantasy. She laid it out for me before I hopped into the shower, and it took all my restraint not to jack-off in there. My dick couldn't get any harder than it is right now.

There's no doubt she heard the shower shut off, heard my footsteps across the tiled floor, but her eyes remain closed. Mine are wide-fucking-open. Standing near the foot of the bed, my gaze is glued to her rocking body, my hearing finely tuned to every wispy breath.

I know how she likes to be touched. How to make her come. Watching her get herself there is still an education.

The soft strokes—a literal petting of that pretty pussy —end as she curls two fingers into her body. It's too dark to see, but I know she's wet. Hot. Tight. Her hips rise to meet the penetration, and the new angle allows her to finger herself deeper. In and out, then she brings those fingers to her mouth and licks between the V they make.

I bite back a groan, but there's no way I can leave my dick alone. I wrap my fist around it, gritting my teeth to resist tugging.

She nestles her fingers between her pussy lips, gasping as she squeezes her clit between them. Another dip into her sweet center, then she rolls the first circle over her clit. A soft touch, but not for long. Each pass is harder, faster, until the circles become a frantic back-and-forth. Her hips tilt upward, her ragged breaths filling the room.

I'm fucking jealous of her fingers, but there's no way

I'm *catching* her yet. I need to see more. I need to see her come.

"*Troy...*" My name is a soft plea, but I know she's not talking to me. She's talking to the version of me in her fantasy. A wordless, sexy-as-fuck moan leaves her lips, her hips jerking wildly beneath her touch as she comes.

Fuck, I need to be in that fantasy. Now. For real.

She pulls her hand away when my weight dips the mattress, her eyes popping open, as if I've truly just caught her. As if we didn't plan this little show. "Did you—" Her eyelids flutter rapidly as she pulls her bottom lip between her teeth. "Were you watching me?"

Looks like we're staying in fantasy mode.

"I saw every sexy second." I slide my palms up the insides of her legs, then spread them, and wedge myself between her toned thighs. "Tell me what you were thinking about while you were rubbing this pretty little pussy."

Her eyes open wider. "I can't." Either she's legitimately embarrassed, or one hell of an actress.

"You said my name. You imagined me doing something to you. Tell me, and I'll make it a reality."

"It's embarrassing." Her voice is as soft as the skin I'm stroking. "You'll laugh."

This had better be part of the act, because if she believes I'd ever laugh at her private thoughts, I've really fucked things up with her. "I'd never laugh at you. You're too important to me."

"I am?"

Fuck, I wish I knew if she's playing or serious. Going to cover the bases, either way. "You have no idea how much you mean to me." I stroke her cheek, comb my fingers through her hair, where it's fanned on the pillow. Then lean in and brush my lips across hers in a teasing, too-short kiss.

"Tell me your fantasy. What was I doing to you that made you come? I want to make it real."

"You were fucking me," she whispers. "Fucking me so deep, telling me all the ways you're going to claim me, and..."

"And what, sweetheart? Don't get shy on me now, I want to hear everything."

"It'll be too much."

"There's no such thing with you." I'm fucking putty in her soft little hands. How hasn't she realized this by now? Guess I'm going to have to show her. Keep showing her. One hand curled over her hip, I slide inside, groaning as her pussy hugs me tight. "Fuck, you feel so good. Made just for me." I rock my hips, eliciting a gasp when I hit her G-spot. "That's right. Your body sings for me, only for me. I'm the only man who gets to make you come."

"Forever," she says, digging her nails into my butt as I grind against her clit. "Tell me it's forever."

"It's forever." I pull out, then fill her up again, burying my dick deep. "Never going to let another man have you." No holding back now. I'm all in, in every way. Shooting my heart out of my mouth as I fuck her deep and hard. "Going to fill every part of you with my dick. Watch you swallow every drop when I blow down your throat."

"God, yes," she pants, between thrusts.

My balls are already high and tight, ready to unload. I shift to my knees, tilt her hips upward, so I can rub her clit, get her where I need her. "This sweet pussy is mine. Your virgin ass is mine. Your heart is mine. Every part of you is mine."

"All of me, forever." She breathes the word, tits heaving and thighs shaking. *"Troy..."* My name rides the world's sexiest moan. Then she's bucking against me, her pussy squeezing me tight as she comes.

"Fuck, baby, fuuuck…" Crushing my lips against hers is the only thing that stops me from telling her I love her. But I want to. I really fucking want to.

seven

CRICKET

"WHAT ABOUT THIS ONE?" I tilt my head, holding the red sunhat in place while giving him a cover-girl pose.

"You look beautiful, baby." Some guys might say that because they're tired of shopping with their wife or girlfriend. Not Troy. The smile on his face and his laidback-yet-attentive presence tells me he's happy to watch me try on a dozen more hats, or anything else that catches my eye in the town's open-air market.

As I've done for the last hour. I return the hat to the vendor, thanking the woman for her time before joining Troy, where he's leaning against a tree. "Okay, I've subjected you to enough hats and dresses. What would you like to look at?"

"You." His hungry gaze drifts down my body, as if he's mentally undressing me.

Beneath the thin cotton sundress, my nipples are hard enough to cut glass. I assume a posture that pushes my breasts up and out. I know he loves my boobs, and I'll take every bit of that attention. Especially since I don't know what will happen once the lump is diagnosed. But that's not a today thought, so back in the box it goes.

"I'm serious," I say when his gaze works its way back to my face. "There must be something you'd like to shop for."

"There is. More things for you." He pushes off the tree, banding an arm around my waist and pulling me in tight. "Why didn't you get a hat?"

"I don't need one."

He's smart enough to read between the lines, and based on the stern set of his eyebrows, he's not a fan of the subtext. His arm slides from my waist and he clasps my hand, then leads me back to the market stall. "We'll take the red hat she just had on. And the white one she tried on first, too."

"Troy, that's—"

"Careful, beautiful," he says, taking cash from his wallet. "If you say 'too much,' I'm going to walk back through the market and buy every single thing you touched."

"Why?"

"Because he *loves* you, girl." The vendor beats him to an answer, beaming as she places the red hat on my head. "Anyone with eyes can see this man in deep with you, and that's right where he wants to be."

Troy chuckles while handing her several folded bills. "Thanks."

My heart is racing in my chest, beating so hard, I wouldn't be surprised if they can see it. After the things Troy said to me a couple hours ago, while he was inside me, I can't help hoping the market vendor is right. Because while he didn't confirm that he loves me, he didn't deny it, either. And, God, it feels like he loves me.

"Let's go back to the resort," I say, once we're out of the vendor's earshot. "I'll model the hat for you in our room."

Once again, he's smart enough to get my gist. This time, his eyebrows rise, rather than draw together. "Just the hat?"

I turn my head and smile up at him. "Well...I think it'd look good with my red shoes from last night, don't you?"

"I think if you're standing in front of me wearing nothing but a hat and heels, we're not going to make it to the nightclub tonight."

"What if I'm not standing? What if I'm kneeling, or bent over the edge of the bed?" I gasp as he jerks me off the path, leads me behind the row of merchant stalls, then presses me against a tree.

"I can't get enough of you." He wedges his quadriceps between my legs. Cups my nape as roughly as the bark at my back. "I'm never going to get enough."

"Good," I whisper, before his lips seal to mine. Then I'm lost to his kiss, sucking his tongue when it strokes into my mouth, moaning as he kneads my ass through the thin cotton. I never liked public displays of anything with the guys I dated. Troy could hike up my dress and fuck me right here, where anyone could see, and I wouldn't just let him, I'd love every minute.

That doesn't happen though. He breaks the contact as quickly as he initiated it. His eyes are dark with arousal, his nostrils flared, but his brow line is tightly furrowed as he gently smooths my rumpled dress.

"You didn't have to stop."

"I shouldn't have started," he says, crossing his arms over his chest. "You deserve better than some manhandling and groping behind a shack."

"I happen to love it when you manhandle and grope me, whether it's behind a shack, on horseback, poolside, or anywhere else." I commandeer one of his hands and mold it to my breast. "Grope me, hunky husband. I want you to."

His laugh attracts the attention of the nearest vendor, who peers at us from around the side of their stall. Troy clasps my hand, weaving our fingers together. "Let's go back to our room, where I can give you a thorough groping."

"And a manhandling?"

"Whatever you want, beautiful wife."

"Really?"

He nods while lifting our joined hands, then points at my pinky finger. "See this right here? I'm wrapped around it. And like the hat-lady back there said, I'm right where I want to be."

CRICKET

Every minute at the resort with Troy was amazing, but the last couple of days...God, they were the best of my life. Two days packed with nonstop attention from the man I love.

He promised to worship me, and he kept his promise. Endless kissing, holding hands, hugging, dancing, and sex. God, the sex. I lost track of how many times he made me come. I'm not even sure I could accurately count the number of times we had sex, because one time melded into another and another, every hour we were naked together.

He kept his promise to ruin me, too, but not in the way he thinks.

I'll only think of him while I'm getting fucked, because I'll never be with another man. I didn't want to be before, and there's no way I could be now.

He's been quiet since we checked out of the resort this morning. The walls that finally crashed and turned to dust a couple days ago have reappeared, getting higher as we head toward home. By the time we exit the highway, his relaxed expression is completely gone, replaced by a clenched jaw and shuttered eyes.

I've already asked if he's okay. Twice. He claims fatigue. Totally reasonable, given we've barely slept for two days. Nonstop sex has to take a toll, even on a man as virile as Troy.

But there's more to his mood shift than fatigue. If that's all it was, he'd still be holding my hand. Kissing me every chance he gets. Smiling at me.

He hasn't touched me since we got in the car. Hasn't glanced at me during the drive from the airport. He's sitting in the seat beside me, but he might as well be a million miles away.

Exhaling, I let my head fall back against the backrest.

"Everything okay?" Troy asks, breaking his apparent vow of silence. The weight of his stare compels me to turn my head. He's still sporting the serious expression he chose for the return trip, but his eyes swirl with concern. It's a start.

"Just lamenting our return to reality."

"I feel the same way."

I grab the kernel and pour a bucket of hope on it. "I had the best time with you," I say, settling my hand on his muscular leg. "Every minute of it, even the ones you were being a pussy-tease."

His deep, manly laugh fills the car, a smile finally breaking the strain that's been cemented on his face all day. "Pussy-tease. That's a new one."

"Yes, well, don't even *think* about going back to reclaim the title. I mean, you can tease—I do enjoy it when you tease—as long as you don't leave me hanging too long. Mrs. Mannington has needs and expectations only her husband can meet."

Darkness descends on his expression. "Yeah, I guess we should've talked about this already."

Doom swirls in my abdomen, tries climbing upward, into my chest. Not so long ago, I would have let it. Everything is different now, and I have no intention of backsliding. Time is precious. Our relationship is too amazing to give up.

"I could ask 'talk about what?' but I'm not dense. You've been giving me the chilly treatment since we left the resort. Are you breaking up with me?"

"We'll still be married," he says, focusing on the road ahead. "For as long as you need to be."

"And if I say that's forever?"

Still watching the road, he grunts. "You won't need me forever. Once we get your medical stuff taken care of, you'll be good to get on with your life."

"If that's your nice-guy way of telling me to get out of *your* life, please say it directly. Tell me our trip was a fun fuckfest, but you don't want me as your wife, and you want to end the marriage the first chance you get."

He glances over, long enough to meet my gaze with storm-filled eyes. "I'm not saying that."

"Because you don't want to hurt my feelings?" I huff

when he looks away without answering. "Is it because I won't be pretty and sexy if I lose my hair, and maybe my breast?"

That makes him look at me again. Makes him glare. "Are you fucking kidding? You think I'm that much of a superficial asshole?"

The piercing force of his stare steals my tongue, so I answer by shaking my head.

He blows out a long breath, his knuckles turning white as he grips the steering wheel and returns to looking at the road. "It's complicated."

"Only for you."

The tension between us is palpable—and entirely new. I hate it. Enough to make tears blur my vision. I control them by tilting my chin up. Hide them by looking out the passenger window, though I see nothing as Troy makes the final handful of turns that ultimately end in his driveway. We're home. Only I don't know what that means.

He gets out, moving around quickly to open my door, but escapes having to touch me by loading himself with all the luggage. "You can go in the house," he says, closing the SUV's rear hatch.

Not-so-subtle hint taken, I semi-stomp up the pavement, probably looking more like a petulant child than a honeymoon bride. I stop on the stoop, turning to confront him, but don't get a word out before the front door whips open.

"Welcome home!" Gina bursts through the opening to tackle-hug me. "Wow, look at you... Did you even go in the sun? You barely got a tan."

"I used lots of sunscreen." I take a chance and shoot a smile over my shoulder at Troy. "Didn't I?"

"Yeah," he says, edging around us. "Excuse me, ladies. Going to take these bags in, then mow the lawn."

Seconds later, I'm inside the house with my best friend. The lawnmower fires up in the backyard, and it takes everything in me not to cry.

"Okay, what's going on?" Gina asks, because I couldn't fool her if I tried. "I thought you guys would have a good trip. I knew it might be a bit weird, with it being just the two of you, but you've always gotten along really well, and you're both fun, laidback people. What happened?"

There's no point trying to hide it from her. She's my best friend. For the next however long I'm here, she's going to be my housemate. She'll either figure it out, or hound it out of me. I might as well tell her straight-up.

"I, um, we, uh..." So much for being direct. I can't tell her. "Everything went great. But we kind of had an argument on the way home."

"Aw, shitty way to wind down your vacation. Whatever it was about, I'm sure it'll pass. I can't imagine it was anything important, right?"

"Right," I say, nodding. Lying. Something I hate doing, especially with Gina.

"Why don't you grab a hot shower to get rid of the travel grime, and I'll order a pizza. We can pig out and have a couple drinks while you tell me all the dirty details of the hottest guy you saw at the resort."

I cough, practically choking on my own tongue. "I will grab a shower, but I'm going to bail on the rest. I could use a good night's sleep."

"Okay." Gina wags a finger at me. "But I get a raincheck on the dirty details."

That conversation is *never* going to happen.

"Oh, hey," she says, as I pick up the suitcase that has my

toiletries. "You'll have to use the shower in my dad's en suite. The one in the main bathroom is broken."

I narrow my gaze when she bites the inside of her cheek, totally failing to hide her smile. "Broken how, and since when?"

"Since Martin spent last week here, and I accidentally pulled the showerhead thingy out of the wall while we were having crazy-hot shower sex."

"Oh my God, you seriously did?" I cover my mouth to mute my snorted laughter.

"I did! And it was ah-mazing. The sex, I mean. Not cleaning the half-flooded bathroom afterward." Her eyes open wide as saucers before she cranks her head toward the rear of the house. "I'm not telling my dad the truth, obviously. He likes Martin, and my dad's no prude, but I doubt he'd want to hear about *that*. If he mentions that I slipped in the shower and grabbed the showerhead cord to save myself, you just nod and look appropriately concerned, okay?"

"Of course." Though, at this point, I doubt he'll mention anything about anything to me.

"What's that for?" she asks when I set my suitcase on the floor and give her a squeezy hug.

"For being my best friend."

"Easiest job in the world," she says, releasing me.

"I hope you always feel that way."

"Why wouldn't I?" The question is barely out of her mouth before she sucks in a shocked breath, grabs my shoulders, and holds me at arms' length. "Oh. My. God." She gives me a head-to-toe once-over, narrowing her gaze when I squirm on the spot. "You didn't get a tan while you were away, you got *laid*. And laid well, based on the color of your cheeks right now."

"A lady never tells?" It's weak, and I know it.

As does Gina, whose burst of laughter probably would've infiltrated the neighbors' kitchen, if not for the lawnmower noise beyond the nearby, open window. "Then we're not ladies, because we *always* tell. Spill it, you. Quickly, before my dad comes in." Her eyes open wide again. "Wait, is that what you argued about on the way home? Is he pissed off because you had sex with someone?"

"Um..."

She makes a stop gesture with one hand. "I'll talk to him."

"Please don't."

"Don't worry, I'll be nice about it. But he needs to remember he's not *your* dad, and he shouldn't act like he is."

"He doesn't act like he's my dad," I say, inching backward and snapping up my suitcase. "Please don't talk to him about this. Or about me, in general. Okay?"

"But I could help smooth things over."

I shake my head. "We need to work through our issues, personally."

"Okay," she says, shrugging. "But I'm around if you need backup. My dad's a great guy, but he can be a stubborn ass sometimes."

Don't I know it.

CRICKET

Troy added the en suite three years ago. He did most of the renovation himself, walking around shirtless for hours at a time, his fine physique glistening with the sheen of hard-working muscles. Good thing Gina never minded me hanging around her house, because I spent every possible minute here that summer.

Who am I kidding? I've spent every possible moment here since day one. For the friendship. The tightknit sense of belonging. To be as close as possible to the object of my infatuation-turned-lust-turned-love.

I've never done more than take a quick peek at the finished en suite until today. Troy did an amazing job. He turned a tiny, adjoining bedroom into his private sanctuary. The huge, walk-in shower has more jets than the whirlpool tub at the resort. It's glorious. And entirely open concept. There's no door, just an archway where his old closet used to be, then a righthand turn into the bathroom.

Vice-versa on the way out, which is where I run into Troy—literally—in all his naked glory.

"Fuck," he says, closing his hands around my bare upper arms. "What're you doing in here?"

"Having a shower. The other one is broken." I don't move.

Neither does Troy. He could step away from me, could grab something, anything, to cover himself with…but he doesn't. Instead, his palms skate downward, until his fingertips meet the edge of my towel, wrapped snugly around my chest. His cock thickens where it's wedged between us, and his nostrils flare. He wants me.

I shift my palms from his chest—where they landed when we collided—to the tucked-in edge of my towel. A gentle tug and it opens, the soft terry fabric sliding as low as our close clinch permits.

"*Cricket.*" My name in his deep voice is a warning. To me. To himself.

Not good enough.

"If you have something to say to me, say it."

His lips form a razor-straight line. "I'm grabbing a shower."

"That's it? That's all you're going to say?"

His nod is as tight as his clenched jaw. He releases me, eating me up with his gaze when my towel drops to the floor. Then he turns and walks away, leaving me alone in his room. Near a bed he's clearly determined not to share with me.

Well, screw that. Until he says the words I don't want to hear—really says them, to my face—we aren't done.

I follow him into the bathroom. Into the shower, where thousands of drops of water are lucky enough to run over his hard, toned body.

"Cricket, what the fuck." There's an edge in his voice that could be anger.

I'll take my chances. I relieve him of the soap, lather it between my palms. Revel in the groan that vibrates from him when I slick my hands over his shoulders, chest, arms... then lower.

"Fuck, your touch is amazing." He widens his stance as I follow the V of his lower abs to the crease where his thigh meets his groin. Another groan rises from his mouth when I caress his balls, slide my fingers over his perineum while stroking the base of his cock with my other hand. "You shouldn't be in here, sweetheart. We shouldn't be doing this."

Sweetheart.

My heart races as I step back. "Then tell me to leave." Our gazes lock as water rinses the soap from his body. "If you truly don't want me here, tell me to leave."

"I can't."

"Because you're afraid I might turn into a crazy stalker if you end things?"

He grunts a laugh. "No."

"Then why, Troy?" I close the gap between us, twining my arms behind his neck while pressing my body tight to his. "Either give me a good reason to leave, or a better one to stay."

Hand tangled in my hair, he tugs me closer, angles my head, and takes possession of my mouth. Each sweep of his tongue is more insistent than the one before. He bands an arm around my leg and raises it, opening me for him.

The air rushes from my lungs when he fills me in one swift stroke. He holds me tight, his groan rumbling against my lips. Then my feet leave the floor as he picks me up. Pinning me between his body and the smooth, tile wall, he pushes deeper. Never withdrawing, he rocks his hips in rhythmic, upward thrusts that set my nerve endings on fire. But it's not enough to take me over, and Troy knows that. He knows all my secrets now. Well...almost all.

"Don't want to give up your mouth, but I need you to come," he says, sliding from my body and returning my feet to the ground. He bands my waist and turns me around. Circling my wrists, he plants my palms against the tile. "Hands stay up here."

"Yes, sir."

A husky rumble fills my ear. "I like the sound of that." His cock presses against the small of my back as he nudges me closer to the wall. "Going to like the sound of you coming more, though." He reaches in front of me to reposition the adjustable jets, then guides his cock home again. "I fucking love being inside you."

"I love it, too." I love *him*. God, he must know I love him.

His hands slide over my body. One settles between my legs, parting my lips so the spray does its rhythmic magic against my clit. "You like that?"

"Yes," I say, rocking against the invisible, watery tongue flicking my sensitive bud. I gasp when Troy cups my breasts, pinching my nipples, first one, then the other. "Harder. I need it harder." Heat flares beneath the next pinch, a drawn-out tug that brings tears to my eyes. "More."

"Fuck." His fingers steal over my clit, rubbing me hard and fast, the way he knows I need. "Fucking come all over me. Squeeze me with your tight little pussy."

Everything goes white as I tumble over, riding his hand and cock until I'm shaking from head to toe.

"Fuck, baby, fuuuck..." He sears my neck with a bite that makes me cry out. He fucks me like a feral beast, his hard thrusts filling the room with the wet smacking of flesh.

My desperate panting mixes with his rough grunts, as his fingers relentlessly draw a second orgasmic wave from my heaving body. Thank God he's a rock because I'm wrung out in his arms.

"I have no bones left," I say.

"Me either. But give me a few minutes to catch my breath, and I'm sure I can come up with another one."

Bliss. That's what this is. "Can we go to the bedroom for round two? If we stay in here, we might turn into wrinkly raisin people. We should save that look for our golden years."

He stiffens, and not in the good way he just promised. A

quick kiss to my temple, then he's out of my body, out of my space, and out of the shower.

"What's wrong?" I shut off the water and follow him, leaving a trail of soggy footprints when I forgo a towel. I'm dripping all over his plush, cream carpet, and he's not batting an eye.

This time, my naked body doesn't affect him. He doesn't even look at me while drying off and getting dressed.

"Answer me," I say, as he moves toward the bedroom door. "A few minutes ago, you were telling me you love being inside me, promising me more after you catch your breath. Now you can't get away from me fast enough. You can't just flip a switch like that and expect me not to demand an explanation. I'll chase you down the driveway, naked, if I have to, Troy."

From across the room, I see his knuckles turning white from gripping the door handle. He exhales, long and low, then turns, meeting my waiting gaze with a tight jaw and shuttered eyes. "I offered you support when you couldn't get it anywhere else, and that appreciation became attraction. It's understandable. But I had no right taking advantage of our situation."

"Are you kidding?" There's nothing funny about this conversation, but I can't help laughing. The kind that hangs in the air like an off-key note, and leaves a bad taste on your tongue. "First of all, you're full of shit. We both admitted to a mutual, longstanding attraction. One that started long before the stupid lump in my breast. As for taking advantage of our situation... *I'm* the one who used every opportunity to seduce *you*. And I'm not sorry I did, because we're great together."

"In bed. We're great in bed."

Even though he's seen every naked inch of me, from every imaginable angle, I've never felt more exposed. "I can't believe you said that."

"I hate hurting you."

"Then don't." I'm practically yelling now, but anger and desperation aren't enough to keep my tears at bay. Two fat ones roll down my cheeks.

"It doesn't feel like it right now, Cricket, but what I'm doing now...it's the right thing."

"For who, you? Because it's not the right thing for me."

He doesn't answer. Not with words. But his guard slips, revealing all the soul-deep emotions he's shared before this horrible moment.

Hope takes a beat in my chest. Then plummets to the depths of my churning gut as he turns and walks out the door.

I wait for the sound of his car leaving before I fall apart completely. Sobs rack my body as I pull on underwear and one of his t-shirts, then slide between the tightly tucked sheets of his bed. I'm not supposed to be here, as he so readily pointed out. Well, fuck that. And him.

"Hey." Gina's voice floats in from the doorway. "I heard everything. I'm not going to ask if you're okay because obviously, you're not."

I pull the duvet over my head as she sits on the edge of the bed. "I'm sorry."

She tugs the blanket to my chin, forcing me to meet her eyes. "For what? Having sex with my dad, not telling me you're having sex with my dad, or for scarring my eardrums for life when I heard you having sex with my dad, because you didn't give me a warning that I need to protect myself from that impending live-porn trauma?"

Miserable as I am, I can't help snorting. "No, yes, and yes. And thank you."

"You're welcome. Now, what can I do to help, because it sounds like my two most favorite people in the world have really made a mess of things."

The sheets are even nicer than the ones at the resort, but I use them to wipe my tears anyway. "Things shouldn't be a mess. We have a great connection. When we're together, it's—"

Gina stops me with a raised hand. "Nope. The first rule of 'You're Fucking My Dad Club' is, you never mention any details about fucking my dad."

Another snorted laugh bubbles out. I'm so lucky to have her as my friend. "I was going to say, when we're together, it's so right. As if nobody else exists, and there's no reason for us *not* to be together. I know he feels the same way, he said a lot of things while we were away."

"Did he tell you he loves you?" she asks, her eyes popping wide.

"Not in those words." God, I wish he'd said those three little words. "But I'm sure he wasn't lying when he said the other things."

"Solid assumption. My dad's a straight-arrow kind of guy. Sometimes he's guarded, sometimes he's a bit too direct, but he doesn't lie."

"Right. And after the stuff he said while we were away... I don't understand why he's backpedaling now."

"He told you why. He thinks he's doing the right thing, and my guess is, he thinks it's the right thing *for you*. And," her eyebrows rise, so do her hands, as if she's surrendering, "I know you don't want to hear this, but maybe he's right."

I sit up, pulling a pillow into my arms and squeezing it. "He's not."

Gina's lips form a wavy line. "He's almost forty, and you just turned twenty-three. You've got school to finish, a career to launch, and you might want kids someday. That's down the road for you, maybe in ten years? He'll be fifty by then. I know he's healthy and fit, but that's still pretty late in life to be starting back at square one with a baby. I'm speculating, obviously, but I know my dad. He's a planner, always thinking six steps ahead. He's had to, since my mother stepped out of the picture when I was still in diapers."

"That's part of why I love him, Gina. One of the many reasons I've been falling in love with him since the day I met him." A fresh stream of tears slides down my face. "I can't turn those feelings off. I don't want to."

"I know, sweetie." The fluffy pillow buffers the closeness of our hug, but not the length. She hangs on, letting go only when my sniffling ends. "You need to focus on *you* right now, and sort out this shit with him later."

I nod because she's right. That doesn't mean I'll be able to follow her advice, but I'll try. Starting with leaving the bed my heart knows I should be sharing with Troy.

The spare bedroom is across the hall. I've slept in it more times than I can count over the years. I always loved being that close to him. Now, it's entirely too far away.

TROY

THE TIME since returning from our trip has been the worst of my life. And that's saying something, because I've lived through some shit. The former times were a struggle because they were unplanned, beyond my control. This dumpster fire is my fault. One-hundred fucking percent. Knowing I did what's best for Cricket doesn't make the fallout easier.

I haven't had to shut her down again. Haven't had to see the pain I've caused reflected in her pretty eyes. The house isn't big, but our paths haven't crossed once since our blowout in my bedroom. She's only "home" when she has to be, and those hours are spent behind the spare bedroom's closed door, across the hall.

Every night, when it's late and the house is quiet, I hear her crying behind that door. That pain is my fault, and it fucking guts me. A lifetime of working hard to be the best man I can down the drain, because I couldn't keep my hands to myself and my dick in my pants. Because I stole her happiness and replaced it with a broken heart. I deserve every shitty fucking thing that happens to me, for the rest of my life.

She deserves the opposite. I'm not a religious man, but I've done some praying. I've offered my life and my soul— or what's left of it—to whatever power can get Cricket through this shit she's been dealt, as quickly and painlessly as possible. Haven't had any takers on my offer yet, but I keep sending up signals. Whatever I have to do.

For now, I'm silently taking care of her, and she's letting me. She's living in my house. Eating my food, even jotting things she wants on the grocery list. She took the insurance and credit cards I left on the kitchen table. Didn't take the note that went with them, but at least she took both cards. I wasn't sure how she'd feel about having *Mrs. Cricket Mannington* embossed on a credit card.

She hasn't used it yet, but I like knowing she'll never be stuck without the means to pay. For anything, ever, because I'll never ask for that card back. Even after the medical stuff is in her past. Even after I'm in her past.

As long as she lets me, I'm going to take care of her. And yeah, I like that if she pulls that credit card out, she's marked as my wife. I'm still a possessive bastard. I still want her, despite cutting her loose. It's fucked up. *I'm* fucked up.

"This is Troy," I say, picking up when the ringing phone on my desk snaps me back to the present.

"Hello, Mr. Mannington, this is John from credit services, calling about a pending charge on the new card issued to your account."

Could be a scam, but it'd have to be a good one for them to get ahold of my direct line at work. Even if the call is bogus, it's still a hell of a coincidence. I lean back in my chair and tap the end of my pen on the desktop. "I'm listening."

"Thank you, sir. The card ending in 1396, issued to Mrs. Cricket Mannington hasn't been activated, but someone attempted to use it at Eastridge Hospital."

I'm on my feet so fast, my pen rattles to the floor, and the back of the chair thuds against the wall. "When?"

"Just now, sir. Would you like us to cancel the card and issue a new one?"

"No. Approve the transaction and activate the card." It's all I can do not to curse and bite the guy's head off.

"I'm sorry, the transaction was declined automatically. We can't approve it at this point. But I can activate the card for you now if you'd like."

Fuck. "Do that, thanks. Do you need anything else?"

"No, sir. That's all. Thank you for choosing—"

I hang up before the guy can finish his customer-service spiel. Then I'm out, tossing, "Family emergency, I'll check in with you later," to my assistant in the outer office, along with, "And find out why Cricket's benefits card isn't working."

Every eye in the room follows me as I storm toward the door. I hope my emergency comment is an exaggeration. I shouldn't be in the position of hoping, of not knowing why Cricket's at a hospital. Whatever the reason, I should already be there, by her side. I would be, if I hadn't pushed her away.

The second I'm in the car, connected to the Bluetooth, I call her. Four rings later, I get her voicemail. "End call," I say before her soft voice reaches the end of her recorded message. Either she's ignoring me, or she's unavailable to answer. I hope to fuck it's the first thing.

Traffic is thick, and it takes twenty minutes to get to the hospital. Another five to find a parking spot. I'm outside the main entrance when it hits me—I don't know where to go from here. In more ways than one.

I pull up Gina's contact and hit the Call button, barking at her the instant we get connected. "Cricket's at Eastridge Hospital. Do you know why?"

"Yes."

If she wasn't my daughter, I'd lose it. More than I already have. I close my eyes and take a breath. Regroup. Focus. If Cricket was hurt, or in trouble, Gina would have called me. I need to get my shit together. Everything is going to be fine.

Gina's heavy sigh drifts through the speaker. "She's there for a biopsy."

"What?" Everything is *not* fine. "Why didn't someone tell me about this? I had to find out she's at the hospital from the fucking credit card company. Do you know what time the appointment is, or what floor it's on?"

"Geez, Dad. For a guy who doesn't want to be part of her life, you sure are worked up about being excluded from it."

"Gina Marie, this isn't the time for your attitude. You're not too old to be grounded."

"And you're not too old to have a happy, long-lasting marriage with Cricket. Think about that on your way to the second-floor C-wing."

"Thanks." That's all I've got right now. There's no time to have this conversation with my daughter. I hope to hell there's still time to have it with Cricket.

TROY

I'm grateful for Gina's hint, but there are a lot of doors in the C-wing, and I'm on the fourth one before I find Cricket.

Her eyes open wide at the sight of me. She doesn't speak when I take the seat beside her. Doesn't resist when I take her hand and thread our fingers together. But she doesn't smile either. Doesn't turn to look at me. Neither of which I deserve.

"I should've been here from the start," I say. "Here and any other appointments I've missed. I should've been with you every step of the way."

"It's fine." Her voice is quiet, her gaze focused on the wall across the room. "I didn't expect you to come to my appointments, or...anything."

Because I was a huge asshole. A stupid fucking bastard.

"Cricket," a nurse says, opening an inner-office door. "We're ready for you."

I rise along with Cricket, squeezing her hand tighter when she tries moving away. "Wait." Meeting the nurse's gaze, I ask, "Would it be possible for me to have a minute with my wife before she goes in? I'm sorry to hold you up, I was late getting here. I promise it won't take long."

"Of course." The nurse nods at me, then at Cricket. "Come back when you're ready."

There's a woman in the small waiting room, another behind the counter built into the interior wall. Not an optimal setting for what I need to say, but that's on me.

I take Cricket's second hand and bring us face-to-face.

"I thought setting you free would be the best thing for you, in the long run. But I was an asshole, treating you the way I did, and I've spent every minute since regretting hurting you. I was wrong to take the decision from you. It's ours to make, not mine. I don't deserve another shot, but I'm asking for one. Let me be here for you. With you. As your husband, for as long as you'll have me."

"You want to stay married?" she whispers. "Really married?" Her beautiful eyes turn glassy when I nod.

I need to make sure that sheen is from impending happy tears. I drop to one knee and stare up at this woman who owns my fucking heart. "I love you, Cricket. I'm crazy in love with you. I'd be the luckiest man on earth if you'd marry me, again. Because you want to this time. Be mine. Every day, for the rest of our lives."

A smile that could light the world—it definitely lights up mine—breaks across her face. "Yes," she says, head bobbing. She gasps when I scoop her off her feet while rising. "Are you sure?" Her soft voice slides into my ear while I'm hugging her. "If this is because of the biopsy—"

"It's because I need you. I don't know how I lived without you before, but I don't want to do it anymore. Let me spend forever showing you how much I love you."

"I love you too," she says, burying her face against my chest when I return her feet to the ground.

It's not the place for the kiss I want to give her. *Need* to give her. I tip her chin up and settle for one that's PG-rated. Except, it's never settling when I'm with her. It's fucking everything. Even the small taste sends blood rushing to my dick. I press it against her, smiling against her lips when her breath catches.

Someone clears their throat behind me. A subtle time's-up.

I drop a kiss on her nose while easing back. "Can I go in with you, hold your hand during the procedure?" I force myself to remain calm when she shakes her head. "Then I'll be right here, waiting to take you home."

To our home. To our bed. To our future.

epilogue

CRICKET

BEYOND THE HEAVY DOUBLE DOORS, the church's organist begins playing *A Thousand Years*. The notes tug at the corners of my mouth, drawing it into a smile that chases the nerves away.

"Whatever makes you happy, sweetheart," were Troy's exact words when I asked if he'd be okay with a non-traditional wedding march. That's his answer to everything. The best part is, he's not saying it out of disinterest. He truly means the words.

In the eight months we've been married, he's shown me, over and over, how much he values my happiness. How much he loves me. After my cancer diagnosis, he held me, let me soak him with tears, night after night. He was by my side through pre-op, the lumpectomy, and radiation appointments. The surgery hasn't changed the way he looks at me—or how much he wants me. He still worships my boobs every chance he gets. Both of them. The scarred, misshapen one gets as much of his hungry attention as its fully intact partner.

"It's time." Gina squeezes my hand before stepping forward to open the doors. She's wearing a pink bridesmaid dress this time around. Breast-cancer-ribbon pink, to be exact. Her choice. My best friend looks beautiful. I couldn't love her more if I tried.

Every eye in the packed church turns toward Gina. Then, once she's reached her position to one side of the altar, those eyes are all on me. The weight of their stares barely registers as I walk down the aisle. No, as I *float* down the aisle, toward my husband. He's all I see. The way he's watching me, I know I'm all he sees, too.

Some people think this wedding doesn't mean anything. They couldn't be more wrong. Our first ceremony was intense, exciting, and perfect. Today's is steeped in deep emotion. It's perfect too, in a different way. A celebration of our unexpected, resilient, unstoppable love.

"Jesus, you're so fucking beautiful."

I can't help giggling when the minister chokes at Troy's language. "You're pretty fucking hot, yourself."

Behind me, Gina mumbles something that sounds very much like, *Get a room*, before she reaches over to divest me of my bridal bouquet. Then it's showtime. But not for the dozens of family, friends, and whomever else Troy stuffed into the church because he wanted the whole world to see us this time. This showtime is for us.

The first time we swore our vows before God, we didn't expect them to last. Neither of us realized the other's true feelings, or fully accepted our own. We didn't appreciate the promises made in those vows. We do now. Saying the same words today, looking into each other's eyes, hearts, and souls, is a new beginning and a homecoming, rolled into one.

"You may kiss your wife," the minister says, adjusting the traditional statement to fit our situation.

"I love you, sweetheart." Troy cups my face, his clear, adoring gaze locked with mine. "Forever."

"I love you too." I barely get the words out before his mouth seals to mine. The rest of the world fades away with the first sweep of Troy's tongue. His moan rumbles through me, straight to my core. Arms twined behind his neck, I press myself against him, as close as two fully clothed people with a roomful of onlookers can get.

This time, Gina's, "Get a room!" is at full volume, and it evokes laughter, whistling, and clapping from our guests.

My face is flushed with heat when we break the kiss. Not from embarrassment, though. The heat is entirely Troy's doing. "What do you say, hot husband? Should we skip the reception and move straight to the honeymoon?"

To my surprise, he shakes his head. "No way I'm giving up the chance to dance with my beautiful wife in her fairy-tale-princess dress."

"I do feel like I'm living a fairytale. Thank you for being the handsome prince who swept in and claimed me."

His smile gets a wicked-sexy edge. "I've got a lot more *claiming* in store for you, Mrs. Mannington. It's going to be fucking hot in Jamaica next week."

"Then hurry up and take me to the ball, Mr. Mannington, so we can get to the hot honeymoon fucking."

His husky laugh ripples through me, then my feet leave the ground as my sexy, alpha prince twirls me around, right there in front of everyone. Happily-ever-after isn't just for fairytales.

Thank you for reading Wedded Miss! I hope you enjoyed this steamy and sweet, forbidden romance. I'd be so grateful if you have a few minutes to leave a review or rating on BookBub, Goodreads, or wherever you purchased this book.

XO
~ KARLA

If you love age-gap romances, check out
The Deal With Love for your next steamy read!

Join Karla's mailing list to stay up-to-date on
all of Karla's new releases, sales, and more.
www.karladoyle.com/newsletter

about the author

A small-town girl with some big-city experience, Karla resides in South-western Ontario with her husband and two children. She studied fashion design in college and spent 20+ years working in that industry before succumbing to the writing muse. When she's not writing the sexy stories that swirl around in her head, you can find her cuddled up with a book and her adorable pets.

Karla loves hearing from readers! Connect with her online, or send her an email: karla@karladoyle.com.

Join Karla's mailing list to stay up to date on all her news.
www.karladoyle.com/newsletter

facebook.com/KarlaDoyleAuthor

bookbub.com/authors/karla-doyle

goodreads.com/karlad

youtube.com/KarlaDoyleAuthor

tiktok.com/@karladoyleauthor

also by karla doyle

Wedded Miss

Dad Bod Wingman (Hope Harbor)

Heart Beats (Hope Harbor)

Last Call Casanova (Hope Harbor)

Fleshing It Out (Hope Harbor)

The Deal With Love (Hope Harbor)

Doggy Style (Hope Harbor)

Resorting to Love (linked to Hope Harbor)

White Lie Christmas (linked to Hope Harbor)

King of Her Dreams (Hope Harbor)

Heart of Texas (linked to Hope Harbor)

Her Pipe Dream (Hope Harbor)

Puck That

Now You See Me (Screaming Woods)

Snake Believe (Screaming Woods)

Once Upon A Beast (Hemlock Woods)

The Beast Within (Hemlock Woods)

Mated to the Minotaur

Shifting Gears (Under the Hood)

Dating the Doubter

Gingerbread Man (Man of the Month: Candy Cane Key)

Just in Queso (Man of the Month)

Unexpected Addition

Rumpled (Dark & Twisted Fairytales)

Room Twenty: Blind Submission (Club Sin New Orleans)

12 Days (Hope Harbor)

Gift Wrapped

Cup of Sugar (Close to Home—Book 1)

Icing on the Cake (Close to Home—Book 2)

Sweet as Candy (Close to Home—Book 3)

Body of Work (Very Personal Training—Book 1)

Worth the Wait (Very Personal Training—Book 2)

Game Plan

More Than Words

Crossing the Line

Visit Karla's website for the most up-to-date list:

www.karladoyle.com